A lone man stood in front of the giant glass that looked out over the mountains.

A man whose brown-eyed gaze watched her from across the room with electrifying intensity. His sheer size and power and strength dwarfed the mountains behind him. But it was his clothes that caught her imagination. A black Stetson dangled from one hand. And a pair of worn Wranglers covered his long, strong legs.

Man, oh man.

Crissy's pulse fluttered and her heart throbbed. What was it about cowboys that made her imagination run wild?

She swallowed hard, drew a steadying breath and took hold of her runaway pulse. It didn't matter how gorgeous the cowboy was. Or that every nerve in her body clanged like a four-alarm fire bell. She'd declared a personal moratorium on men.

Dear Reader,

It's that time of year again—back to school! And even if you've left your classroom days far behind you, if you're like me, September brings with it the quest for everything new, especially books! We at Silhouette Special Edition are happy to fulfill that jones, beginning with *Home on the Ranch* by Allison Leigh, another in her bestselling MEN OF THE DOUBLE-C series. Though the Buchanans and the Days had been at odds for years, a single Buchanan rancher—Cage— would do anything to help his daughter learn to walk again, including hiring the only reliable physical therapist around. Even if her last name did happen to be Day....

Next, THE PARKS EMPIRE continues with Judy Duarte's *The Rich Man's Son,* in which a wealthy Parks scion, suffering from amnesia, winds up living the country life with a single mother and her baby boy. And a man passing through town notices more than the *passing* resemblance between himself and newly adopted infant of the local diner waitress, in *The Baby They Both Loved* by Nikki Benjamin. In *A Father's Sacrifice* by Karen Sandler, a man determined to do the right thing insists that the mother of his child marry him, and finds love in the bargain. And a woman's search for the truth about her late father leads her into the arms of a handsome cowboy determined to give her the life her dad had always wanted for her, in *A Texas Tale* by Judith Lyons. Last, a man with a new face revisits the ranch—and the woman—that used to be his. Only, the woman he'd always loved was no longer alone. Now she was accompanied by a five-year-old girl...with very familiar blue eyes....

Enjoy, and come back next month for six complex and satisfying romances, all from Silhouette Special Edition!

Gail Chasan
Senior Editor

Please address questions and book requests to:
Silhouette Reader Service
U.S.: 3010 Walden Ave., P.O. Box 1325, Buffalo, NY 14269
Canadian: P.O. Box 609, Fort Erie, Ont. L2A 5X3

A Texas Tale

JUDITH LYONS

SPECIAL EDITION

Published by Silhouette Books

America's Publisher of Contemporary Romance

To my sister, Jan Martinez, and my brother,
DL Morgan, who were right there when I needed them.
A clear-down-to-the-bottom-of-my-heart thanks, guys.

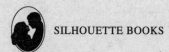 SILHOUETTE BOOKS

ISBN 0-373-24637-4

A TEXAS TALE

Copyright © 2004 by Julie M. Higgs

Visit Silhouette Books at www.eHarlequin.com

Printed in U.S.A.

JUDITH LYONS

lives in the deep woods in Wisconsin, where anyone who is familiar with the area will tell you one simply cannot survive the bitter winters without a comfortable chair, a cozy fireplace and a stack of good reading. When she decided winters were too cold for training horses and perfect for writing what she loved to read most—romance novels—she put pen to paper and delved into the exciting world of words and phrases and, most important of all, love and romance. Judith loves to hear from her readers. You can contact her through her Web site at www.judithlyons.com.

All underlined places are fictitious.

Chapter One

Tate McCade stood in the middle of the Alaskan ski lodge, watching the giant-screen television with the crowd of fifty or so people who'd gathered around for the big event. On screen four women, all blond, all pretty, all wearing daredevil smiles and neon-pink snowsuits prepared to jump out of a helicopter—with nothing but wildly colored snowboards strapped to their feet.

The Alpine Angels were at it again.

Like many of their stunts, this one included lots of snow, rarely traveled mountain peaks and a high degree of risk. Today, the girls were jumping out of the helicopter from fifty feet in the air, each landing on her own mountain and leaving her "signature," the trail left in the pristine snow by her snowboard, on the face of the mountain. The four mountains weren't overly tall, but they were sheer as hell. From the peak to the base, the run was almost straight down.

Damn.

Someone needed to step in and throw a lasso around those ladies and hold tight or none of them would live to see their thirtieth birthdays.

Tate had planned to arrive early enough to lasso at least one of them before she got on that damned chopper. But his flight, like half the flights in the country, had been late. So now, he was stuck here, standing helplessly with nothing but spit and the hope that the women made it to the bottom in one piece.

Tate shifted his gaze from the giant picture to the small family that stood directly in front of the screen. At least there was a halfway decent reason behind this madness. Like most of the other harebrained stunts the Alpine Angels women had performed in the last three years, this one was a fund-raiser. The recipient was the ten-year-old boy sitting in the wheelchair front and center, flanked protectively by his parents. He needed a bone marrow transplant and his family had no insurance to cover the cost.

Tate studied the boy. He was small for his age, pale, and looked as if they couldn't start the procedure any time too soon. But he was a cute kid with a killer smile and there was a sparkle in his eyes that said he was living this minute for all it was worth. If those fool women chose to risk their lives, Tate supposed they couldn't have picked a better reason.

But he wasn't fooling himself. People who pushed the envelope as hard as the Alpine Angels did were usually looking for a way to self-destruct. He hoped to God they wouldn't manage to do it today. It was the last thing the boy needed to see. And besides, Tate had a promise to keep.

He shifted his attention back to the screen. In total surround sound, the whir of the chopper's blades filled the room and vibrated beneath their feet. The scream of the Alaskan wind howled in their ears. It was probably quieter in the damned helicopter. But even over the steady thump in the floor, he could feel his heart pounding, hear it over the roar of the helicopter blades as the first woman moved into jump position.

At the helicopter's open door, the statuesque blonde turned to the camera, smiled and gave a thumbs-up. She took a moment to prepare herself and then jumped into nothingness with a shrieking war cry.

Tate couldn't remember the woman's name, Mattie or Tasha or…something. She wasn't the Alpine Angel he'd come to see. But he held his breath for her, just the same, and prayed for a good landing.

The screen suddenly flashed, splitting into two portions. Three-quarters of the giant picture remained on the three women left in the helicopter. But a separate picture in the upper right hand corner showed the woman who'd just jumped.

She hit the steep face of the mountain hard, snow flying in all directions, completely obscuring her from view. But when the white powder settled she was on her feet, swooshing down the terrain heading for the bottom of the mountain at breakneck speed.

He sighed in relief. One down. Three to go.

The helicopter flew to the next two mountains, dropping a smiling blonde at each, the big screen splitting into more squares with each jump. The three women who'd already made successful landings were screaming down the sheer faces of their mountains in living Technicolor.

Tate shifted his gaze to the left bottom square. The last woman was in place now, leaning out of the helicopter checking the terrain below. Crissy Trevarrow. Or as she knew herself, Crissy Albreit. The woman he'd come to bring home.

She looked back at the camera, her sensuous lips smiling widely, her light green eyes sparkling with excitement and her long curly blond hair blowing in the wind.

His breath caught in his throat and the same sensation he'd gotten the first time he'd seen her picture, not twenty-four hours ago, hit him hard. It was a feeling not unlike one of his wild mustangs delivering a hard kick to the gut. But this sensation was lower, harder and twice as powerful. He wanted her. Like a stallion scenting a mare, he wanted her. Irrational and startling. But undeniable.

And equally unwelcome.

Because Warner Trevarrow, just before he'd died, had made Tate promise he'd not only bring Crissy back to her father's ranch, but he'd make sure she had everything that was good and wonderful and bright. And no matter how you saddled that horse, an ex-con didn't fit into any of those categories.

Fresh powder still clinging to her snowsuit, Crissy gave the boy in the wheelchair a giant hug. "Hey, Chad, what did ya think?" She'd just come in off the mountain, and excitement and adrenaline poured through her system.

The young boy beamed at her, his smile reaching from ear to ear. "Stoking, man. I want to do that some day."

"Yeah, well, I'll tell you what, you get your new bone marrow, spend a year getting strong and this board is waiting for you. Okay?" She handed her snowboard off to his parents, then shot him a teasing smile. "But you start on something a little tamer. Got it?"

The boy nodded. "It's a promise."

"Okay then." She gave him another hug. "Go get 'em, tiger. Listen, I'll be back in a minute. I've got to get something to drink. You want something? Coke? Grape soda?"

The boy shook his head. "Nah. But I want to hear about the run, so hurry back."

"You got it." Smiling, she turned and started through the noisy crowd on her way to the bar. Her run, like the other girls', had been good. Which meant she hadn't fallen and messed up the clean, carved line her snowboard had left in the snow—or broken her neck.

Which also meant the Geneveve Corporation, who'd pledged fifty thousand dollars for each clean "signature," was on the hook for two hundred thousand dollars. Enough to cover the main expense of Chad's bone marrow transplant. Add to that the contributions by the people in this room and the Coopers weren't going to have to sell their home or go bankrupt to save their son. It was a good day.

"Crissy!"

She turned, searching for the caller. She spotted the lodge's owner, his wild red hair flying, pushing his way through the crowd toward her. She waited for him to reach her side, then pitched her voice above the crowd. "What's up, Boyd?"

"A man's looking for you."

She cocked a brow. "Yeah, who?"

The burly owner hooked a thumb toward the lodge's big picture windows.

A lone man stood in front of the giant glass that looked out over the rugged Chugach mountain range. A man whose brown-eyed gaze watched her from across the room with electrifying intensity.

Heat and pure feminine awareness slid through her.

His sheer size and power and strength dwarfed the mountains behind him. But it was the man's clothes, and the way he wore them, that caught her imagination.

A dark blue, western, Saturday-night-let's-go-dancing shirt, complete with black piping and mother-of-pearl snaps, covered his broad shoulders and accented his narrow waist. A black Stetson with a snakeskin band dangled from one hand. A pair of old, but spit-polished, cowboy boots added a few extra inches to his already overwhelming height. And lastly, a pair of worn but spotlessly clean Wranglers covered his long, strong legs.

Man, oh man.

Her pulse fluttered, her heart throbbed. What was it about cowboys that made her imagination run wild?

She swallowed hard, drew a steadying breath and took hold of her runaway pulse. It didn't matter how gorgeous the cowboy was. Or that every nerve in her body clanged like a four-alarm fire bell. She'd declared a personal moratorium on men.

She'd declared it three years ago when she'd found herself living in an apartment she hated and working a job she didn't like any better, all for the sake of a man. A man she'd discovered was sleeping with her on Mondays, Wednesdays and Fridays—and his *other* girlfriend the rest of the week. She'd decided right then she needed to figure out who she was and what she wanted in life. And she obviously needed to do that without having a man around to muddy the waters.

And until this very minute she hadn't regretted that decision. But if she didn't find out what the Marlboro Man wanted and send him right back to his range, that resolution could be in serious jeopardy.

She drew another deep breath. "Okay, Boyd, I got it." Squaring her shoulders, she strengthened her resolve and strode toward the cowboy, ruthlessly ignoring the humming of her nerves as his gaze followed her every move. She stopped a good three feet in front of him—plenty close enough—and tipped her chin up. "Hey, Tex."

An easy smile turned his lips, accenting the fine lines around the corners of his eyes. "What makes you think I'm from Texas?" The words were wrapped in a deep Texas drawl, smooth as silk and sexy as hell.

She chuckled softly, ruefully. "Aren't all cowboys?" At least the ones in her dreams always had been. And since it was obvious Satan was trying to tempt her beyond all reason, this cowboy couldn't have been from anywhere else.

He tipped a shoulder, a self-confident sparkle in his eyes. "The ones worth their salt."

Oh *man*, she was going to be in big trouble fast if she didn't get this good ol' boy on his way. She shook her head and laughed again. "There ya go. Now…what can I do for you? Boyd said you wanted to talk to me."

The teasing light left his eyes, his expression suddenly serious. "I do. And it's important. Is there somewhere quieter we can talk? Somewhere more private?"

A little shiver ran through her. Somewhere quieter? More private? Her room maybe? No way. Besides, she didn't know this man from Adam. So someplace private but close to the crowd would be a wiser choice. She looked around, her eye falling on the closed door next to the bar. She turned back to the cowboy. "How about Boyd's office? I'm sure he won't mind."

"Fine."

"This way." She strode toward the back of the room, dodging the celebrants as she went. She didn't turn around to make sure the cowboy didn't get lost in the crowd. She could feel him behind her. His heat, his intensity, his gaze following her every step.

As she approached the bar, she caught Boyd's eye, pointed to his office door and cocked a brow, asking silent permission to use the room. He nodded and went back to pouring drinks.

She pushed through a small group of revelers that congratulated her and clapped her on the back. She thanked them for coming, for pledging their hard-earned dollars and then quickly excused herself and escaped into Boyd's office.

The cowboy followed her in and closed the door behind him, shutting the party's noise out—and them in.

She backed away from the big stranger, trying to find a space with a little more oxygen. She didn't remember Boyd's office being this small, this close. But it certainly seemed to be now. She took another step back, unzipping the front of her snowsuit. It was warmer in here than she remembered, too. Way warmer. "So, Mr.—I'm sorry, I didn't get your name."

The stranger's gaze snapped up from her waist, the end of her zipper's trek. "McCade." His voice was rough, tight. He cleared his throat, starting again. "Tate McCade." He held out his hand.

She stared at the big, work-roughened hand with its long, strong fingers and calloused palms. No way was she shaking that hand. She didn't want to know just how warm his touch would be. Just how electric. The woman in her was already far too aware of the man's masculine appeal. She turned away and strode to the other side of Boyd's desk. "So what can I do for you, Mr. McCade?"

When she turned back to him, a hint of a smile lifted his lips. Just enough of a smile to tell her she hadn't fooled him. He knew she'd seen his hand and knew why she hadn't shaken it. But that smile quickly disappeared, his brown-eyed gaze turning serious. "I'm not sure how to start this except to say your father sent me."

Her brows crashed together in surprise. "My father?"

He nodded.

Old anger ran through her. She shook her head. "You must have the wrong person. I haven't seen my father since… Well, I don't actually remember ever seeing my father." Bitterness sounded in her voice. "He sent me and my mother packing when I was two."

"That's not quite the way it happened," he said. "And I don't have the wrong person. Your father's name was Warner Trevarrow, correct?"

Apparently, it had been. It was a little fact Crissy had learned when she'd found the name Trevarrow on her mother's marriage certificate and Crissy's birth certificate after her mother's death. When she'd seen that name she'd understood for the first time why she'd never found her father when she'd searched for him under the name Warner Albreit. She'd also understood the care her mother had taken to make sure Crissy never came face to face with her father. And the only reason Crissy could think of for that, was that her mom hadn't wanted Crissy to hear with her own ears that her father didn't want her.

She nodded. "Yes, Warner Trevarrow is my father. Biologically, anyway. The old man certainly was nothing more than a sperm donor. I can't imagine why he'd be looking for me now. Unless—" She shot the cowboy a hard look. "If he's after a portion of the Alpine Angel money you can tell him I don't keep any of it. None of us do. A hundred percent of it is donated. And my job as a waitress at the little pie shop where I live in Denver just barely keeps me in living expenses. I don't have much more money now than my mother did the day he kicked us out on the street."

The cowboy grimaced. "Your father didn't send me to squeeze money out of you."

She raised a skeptical brow. "No? Then why are you here?"

"I'm here because I'm the foreman on your father's ranch. And the executor to his estate."

The executor to her father's estate? The world tilted. Her father was dead? She rocked back, trying to keep her balance, but the room spun and her knees went weak, making her sway on her feet.

Tate rushed around the desk with a soft curse, his arms stretched out to catch her.

She quickly lowered herself into Boyd's chair before he reached her. She definitely didn't need to add the cowboy's touch to her already careening world. She held her hands up to ward away his help. "I'm okay, just…" Stunned.

He dropped his hands to his sides, but his gaze stayed locked on her, watchful, concerned as he stood beside her.

She closed her eyes, blocking him out. Blocking out his intense gaze and his concern and his overpowering maleness as she tried to sift through the emotions swirling inside. Like most kids with a missing parent she'd thought of her father often over the years. On birthdays, she'd wondered if he ever thought of her. Or if he'd wiped her and her mother so completely from his mind, he wouldn't even notice the day.

And she'd had the usual childish dreams of reunion. That her father would wake up one morning and realize what a precious commodity he'd thrown away. That he'd come after them, begging for forgiveness, begging them to return to his life. Promising he'd love them forever and ever.

But mostly she'd thought of Warner Trevarrow in anger. Anger that he'd thrown them out to fend for themselves. Anger that she'd had to watch her mother struggle to keep them fed and clothed and have a roof over their heads. Anger that she'd had to watch her mother die far before her time because they hadn't been able to afford the treatments and medication her mother had needed.

And now this stranger had shown up with the announcement that Warner Trevarrow was dead. She didn't know what to feel. Didn't know whether to be mad or sad or whether she should feel anything at all.

She opened her eyes and met the cowboy's gaze head-on. When she'd first seen the cowboy across the room, she'd feared he would knock her moratorium on men off balance. Now she feared he was about to throw her whole world off balance. Her stomach tying itself into knots, she said, "I think you better tell me what this is all about."

"As the executor of your father's estate—and his friend—I promised to keep your father's spread running until the lawyers found you. And once they found you, I promised to bring you home."

"Home?" The word was a hoarse whisper on her tongue.

"Home to the Big T. Your father's ranch."

Her heart squeezed. "My father owned a ranch?"

Tate McCade nodded, his gaze intensifying, becoming more concerned as he watched her response. "One of the biggest spreads in Texas."

Anger, old and true, began to gather inside her. "My father owned one of the biggest spreads in Texas?" *While my mother and I scraped for every meal we ever ate?*

His gaze turned cautious. "Yes. But it's yours now. *If* you meet the stipulations in the will."

She laughed humorlessly. "Stipulations?" The bastard had washed his hands of her twenty-two years ago. Now he was trying to control her from the grave?

He nodded. "You have to live on the ranch for six

months, full-time, before it becomes yours. At that time, the deed will be signed over to you and you can do whatever you want with it. Keep it. Sell it. Burn it to the ground."

She quirked a brow. "That has a certain appeal."

"Your father wasn't a fool. He thought it might. But he also thought if you spent six months there, you'd come to love it. Love the work and the land. He said his blood ran in your veins, too."

A shiver ran through her. A shiver of pure outrage and revulsion. She pushed herself up from her chair and leaned across the desk. "The man *abandoned* his wife and child, Mr. McCade. I hadn't thought of his blood running in my veins, but now that you've pointed it out, a transfusion doesn't sound like a bad idea. As for the ranch, I don't want it. Not even to burn to the ground. Sorry you wasted your time." She straightened and strode around the desk, heading for the door.

"So you're just going to walk away from it? The ranch? Your father's wishes? Your heritage?" His tone was calm, reasonable, but he wasn't fooling her. She could sense the tension in his body as he pivoted on his heel, tracking her progress.

She stopped with her hand on the doorknob. Her heritage? Her father had kicked her and her mother out of his house—or off his precious ranch, apparently— with nothing but the clothes on their backs. And the few times her mother had tried to contact him for help, he'd refused to take her calls.

Crissy swung back to the cowboy with a feral snarl. "That ranch isn't my heritage. It's my father's attempt to salve his guilty conscience for throwing a helpless woman and a two-year-old child out on the street. His feeble attempt to keep the fires of hell from licking at his boots. Well…I hope those fires burn him to a crisp." She spun back to the door. But before she could slip through, the cowboy's hand landed above her head, pushing the door shut again.

His body loomed over her, his heat soaking into her back, his breath rustling her hair. "You may want your father to burn to a crisp, Ms. Albreit. Hell, maybe you have that right. But before you make a rash decision based on nothing but raw emotion, you might want to think of the broader picture. If you spend six months at the ranch—and still want nothing to do with the place—do you know how many boys just like Chad you could save by selling it instead of burning it to the ground?"

She'd been about to send her elbow into the domineering cowboy's ribs. But now she went still, his words knifing through her anger.

She'd had to stand by, watching her mother suffer through the debilitating and painful symptoms of MS because they couldn't afford the medicine to help control the disease. And she'd had to accept the reality that her mother had died months, possibly years, before her time because she couldn't afford the medical treatments that would have prolonged her life.

She hated the thought of others facing that ugly reality. It's why she'd started the Alpine Angels. Reluctantly, the tight hold she had on the doorknob relaxed.

Sensing her capitulation, McCade backed up. But he didn't go far. Definitely not far enough. She could still feel the coiled tension radiating from his body, still smell his spicy aftershave as she turned around to face him, tipping her head up to meet his gaze.

He watched her through narrowed eyes. He was playing dirty and he knew it. The tight line of his mouth made her think he didn't like it. But the hard core of determination in his eyes told her he'd play even dirtier if necessary.

But she was no pushover. She raised her chin. "You haven't won yet, Mr. McCade. How many Chads?"

"If you sell smart, invest smart, a couple hundred, maybe more."

"A couple hundred?" the surprised exhalation whispered from her lips. Dear God. How could she possibly justify turning her back on that?

A wry laugh echoed through her head. As if she would have turned her back on the deal if she could have saved only one. She sighed in defeat. "All right, Mr. McCade, you've won. Where's this ranch? And how do I get there?"

He pulled two plane tickets from the back pocket of his jeans. "Not a problem. I'll take you."

She stared at the two tickets in his hand. Well, she'd managed to send the cowboy right back to his range, all right. Only problem was, he was taking her with him.

Chapter Two

Tate sat on the 747, his seat belt buckled, his hat resting on one knee, waiting for Crissy to show up for the 9:00 a.m. flight. After he'd spoken to her yesterday afternoon, she'd demanded he hand over her ticket and told him she'd see him on the plane. She had a lot to think about, she'd told him, and she didn't want any disturbances or distractions while she did it.

He hadn't liked the idea, but when he'd tried to reason with her, convince her that he should stay close in case she had any questions, she'd made it clear his presence anywhere near her was a deal breaker. So he'd left the lodge and headed back to his hotel, where he'd spent the rest of the day and most of the night wondering if she'd show up this morning.

It wasn't looking good.

He glanced at his watch. The plane was scheduled to take off in ten minutes, which meant they'd be shutting the hatch and taxiing out to the runway any minute. And Crissy still wasn't here.

Great.

If she didn't show up soon, he'd have to leave the flight to chase her down, which, since he'd been stupid enough to check his damned duffel, would no doubt raise a thousand red flags with airport security. He'd probably find himself locked in a room with ten burly guards determined to prove he was a big terrorist.

Fun.

He glanced at his watch. Again. *Come on, Crissy. Don't let me down. I have an aversion to burly guards with an agenda.*

Just as he was preparing to stand up and walk off the plane, Crissy strode on.

Thank God.

He watched as she made her way down the aisle, doing her best to keep her small bag and purse from bumping the seated passengers. Her shoulders were slumped, a dead giveaway that she'd had a long night. And the slight red rim to her eyes told him she'd spent at least part of it crying. Damn. He wished he knew a little about her so he could make this easier for her. Unfortunately, beyond the fact that her mother had died seven years ago and she was one of the famed Alpine Angels, he didn't know a damned thing.

Since he'd missed the chance to keep Crissy from

jumping out of that helicopter, he wished he'd taken a few extra days to come get her. If he'd waited, the P.I. would have had time to collect more facts on her. And he wouldn't be riding blind now. But he hadn't taken that road. And he'd learned a long time ago you couldn't change the past.

No matter how much you wanted to.

At least the P.I. had promised to fax whatever he found out at the end of each day. Yesterday's and today's reports should be waiting for him by the time they got home.

Crissy finally made it to her seat—the one right next to him. She acknowledged him with a short, curt nod, stowed her bag in the overhead and sat, her shoulder brushing his.

His body completely overreacted to the casual touch, heat and need surging through him. He closed his eyes, ruthlessly stomping on the futile response. A response that would make the next six months damned uncomfortable if he didn't get a handle on it. And soon.

As if sensing his reaction Crissy shifted positions, moving to the far side of her seat, disconnecting their shoulders.

The move didn't surprise him. He knew she felt the sexual awareness that arced between them, too. He'd seen the interest in her gaze when she'd spotted him across the room. Felt the throbbing pulse of intimacy that had enveloped the office when she'd shut the door. Luckily, for whatever reason, she was ignoring the attraction as studiously as he.

Staring straight head, she drummed her fingers on the seat's plastic arms.

She was wound tighter than a rattler ready to strike. And he was pretty sure the energy snapping between them wasn't the only thing responsible for her obvious case of nerves.

He turned to face her, ready to take the bull by the horns. "Long night?"

She looked at him, raising a single delicate brow. "Did you expect anything else?"

"No," he admitted. "That's why I wanted to be on hand. In case you had questions. Or just needed someone to talk to."

"What I really needed was someone to scream at." Her lips twisted unhappily. "Or punch."

He checked the smile that pulled at his lips. Her dad hadn't seen her since she was two, but he'd known her pretty well. Warner had dreamed of finding his daughter and having her run into his arms, thrilled to be united with her old man again. But he'd told Tate on more than one occasion that as much as he wanted that to happen, he didn't expect it to.

"The first time she sees me she'll probably want to tear my heart out," Warner had told him once. And when Tate had asked why, Warner had just shrugged, and said, "Are you kidding? I don't know what her mom has been saying about me all these years, but considering everything, I doubt it's been good. The fact that I've never heard from either of them pretty much bears that out. And, of course, whether their lives have been

good or bad, there's the little fact that I haven't contributed a damned thing to it. She'll want her pound of
flesh for that."

It looked like Warner was right. And because Tate
knew the old man thought she deserved that pound of
flesh, he hooked his thumb toward the back of the plane.
"Would you feel better if you took me in the back and
pummeled me for a while?" Not that he couldn't think
of a far more enjoyable way to dispel the tension in her,
but...

Not an option.

She shot him a dry, challenging look. "What if I
said yes?"

"When the plane's in the air and the seat belt light
goes off I'll be happy to oblige. I can't guarantee the
stewardesses won't round us up, open the hatch and
toss us out. Or that our fellow passengers won't per-
ceive a threat and beat us to death, but I'm willing to
give it a try."

One of her brows arched in surprise. "My, my, my,
you must be a loyal dog. The old man's dead and
you're still willing to take a beating for him."

There was a time when her dog comment would
have gotten her a fight. He wasn't sure that wasn't her
intention now. But he'd learned the hardest way imag-
inable that anger just dug whatever hole you were in
deeper. Besides, he *was* a loyal dog. Warner had
pulled his sorry self out of a deep, deep hole when
everyone else was shoveling dirt on top of him. He
owed the man.

He shrugged and shot her a teasing smile. "I don't know that it's a very good test of my loyalty. I don't imagine you hit very hard."

She huffed. "Don't bet on it. Right now I feel like I could knock out Holyfield."

He did a quick survey of her slight five-foot-four-inch frame. Her small hands. Not a chance in hell. But he didn't dismiss her anger so easily. Anger, he knew, masked pain. If she was ready to take on the heavy-weight champ, she was obviously in a world of hurt.

And how could she be anything else? She believed her father had abandoned her.

"Look, Crissy, there's a lot you need to hear about your mom and dad. About their marriage. About their breakup."

Anger flashed in her eyes. "How would you know anything about my mother and father's breakup? Were you there?"

"No. But I know what your father told me. And—"

"And I know what my mother told me. And trust me, if I'm going to believe anyone's story, it's going to be hers." Dark shadows skidded across her green eyes. "She might have had her faults, but at least she didn't abandon her child. She didn't throw me out to fend for myself on a dark, rainy night with nothing but the clothes on my back."

Neither had her father. But the path to that truth was long and filled with ugly patches. With other passengers already starting to glance in their direction, now wasn't the time to try to get down it. "This isn't the time or place to discuss this. But you have to realize there are two sides to every story. You ought to at least hear your father's perspective on what happened all those years ago. Then you can decide where the truth lies. My guess is you're going to find it smack-dab in the middle of the story your mother told you and the story Warner told me."

She shook her head. "I'm not interested in Warner Trevarrow's excuses, McCade. I know where the truth lies. I lived it as a child growing up. The only thing that interests me is how much money I'll make selling the old man's ranch."

Warner had stipulated she could sell the spread after six months, but it sure as hell hadn't been his intention. He'd wanted his daughter to fall in love with the Big T. He'd wanted her to stay on the place, learn to run it and someday get married and raise her children there. And somehow, Tate had to lead her to *that* decision.

And not just for Warner. The dark shadows in Crissy's eyes, the turmoil he felt boiling in her told him Crissy needed the Big T as much as any of the cowboys on it did. For many of them, it had been a saving grace.

"So, how big is this place?" Crissy asked.

He pulled his thoughts from his musings. "The Big T?"

She nodded.

"Five hundred thousand acres."

Her eyes went wide. "Wow. That is big. That ought to bring in a pretty penny."

He tipped his head. "As I said, one of the biggest in Texas."

"So you did. What kind of ranch is it? Cattle? Horses? Crops?"

He winced. "Crop operations are called *farms*. The Big T is a *ranch*."

"And from that tone of voice I take it ranches are superior."

He shrugged. "Not superior, really. It's just that… Well, there are farmers and then there are ranchers."

She rolled her eyes. "This is a macho, mine's-bigger-than-yours thing, isn't it?"

He just smiled.

"Yeah, that's what I thought." She shook her head. "So now that we've established the Big T *doesn't* raise crops, how about cattle and horses?"

He nodded. "The Big T raises both."

"Really?" A glint of interest sparked in her eyes. "What kind of horses?"

So, Crissy Albreit liked horses. Good. That would be the hook he'd use to connect her to the ranch then. "Quarter horses. The Big T raises the best working cow ponies in the state of Texas. Do you ride?"

She shook her head. "No. But there'll be plenty of time to learn in the next six months. There certainly won't be anything else to occupy my time."

"Think again. Ranches are busy places. There are fences to keep up. Herds to move from one pasture to another. Branding. Vaccinations. The work is endless."

"Well, I certainly won't be doing any of it."

"Of course you will."

"Of course I won't. I don't know anything about cows or horses."

"You'll learn."

She shook her head. "Little point in that when I'll be selling the place in six months."

He had to change that attitude quick. Not just because he'd never get her to stay on the Big T if she stayed locked in the house letting the anger for her father fester. But because there was nothing better for healing pain and anger than a long ride on a smooth horse over acres and acres of open land. Crissy Albreit needed that.

Needed to begin to heal the anger inside her before the odds caught up with her and she jumped out of one helicopter too many. "You're going to have to involve yourself a little if you intend to have anything worth selling at the end of that six months. Running a big ranch takes a lot of work, a lot of involvement. If you don't take the bull by the horns you're going to have nothing but straggly pastures and dead livestock to sell."

She shot him a skeptical glance. "You've been running the Big T since my father's death, right?"

"Yes, but—"

"Pastures getting straggly?"

"No."

"Any dead cows lying around?"

"No," he said emphatically. "But I'm just the foreman of the ranch, not the boss. You're the boss now.

It's your job to make sure everything is running smoothly."

"Fine. As your boss I'm instructing you to keep on as you have since my father's death, making the best decisions for the ranch without consulting me or waiting for any decision on my part whatsoever." She shot him a sugary sweet smile. "Any questions?"

He shot her a saccharine smile of his own. "Just one. Do you really think I'm going to let you sit on your cute little derriere while everyone else at the ranch works *their* tail off?"

She smiled that sugary sweet smile again. "Of course I do. I'm the boss, right?"

"So you expect everyone on the ranch to work while you sit in the big house twiddling your thumbs?"

"I don't know why anyone at the ranch would care if I was twiddling my thumbs or painting my toenails. I'm a nonentity to them."

He smiled. "Never lived on a working ranch, have you?"

"Obviously not. After all, my father kicked me off when I was two."

He let the angry retort slide. "Well, a working ranch is a little like a small town. There's no such thing as a nonentity. Within days of your arrival everyone will know everything there is to know about you. And they're going to expect you to pitch in and work, just like they are. Your father might have been the owner of the ranch, but he saddled a horse and headed out to the range every day just like every other man on the ranch."

"Oh yeah, bring him up. That'll get me to pitch right in. Besides, why on earth would you or anyone else care if I pitched in or—wait a minute." Her eyes narrowed to suspicious little green slits. "Did my father want me to learn how to run the ranch? Is that why you're pushing so hard? To fulfill another one of my father's requests?"

Damn. He'd stepped into a sinkhole. And he could feel it sucking at his feet. "Maybe I think that sitting in your room sulking wouldn't be good for you. And the fresh air of the open range would be."

"Maybe you do. But that's not what I asked." She looked him right in the eye. "Did my father want me to learn to run the ranch? Maybe hoping I'd fall in love with the place and decide to keep it?"

He wanted to deny the question flat out. But there were rules on the Big T. Not lying was one of them. "Yes," he admitted through clenched teeth, feeling that sinkhole pull him under.

"Well then, cowboy," she said in a voice almost as syrupy sweet as her smile. "You can bet your own cute little derriere that I will let myself be skinned alive before I lift so much as a finger on that ranch." She snatched the hat from his knee, leaned back in her chair and placed the black Stetson over her face.

Conversation over.

He leaned back in his own chair, stifling a groan. Perfect.

Just damned perfect.

Chapter Three

Crissy sat in the big truck next to the cowboy as the sun leaned toward dusk. They'd spent all morning and part of the afternoon hopping from one plane to the next. And the rest of the day in this truck, rolling over mile after mile of highway. She was tired and edgy and…

Terrified.

She didn't know what she was terrified of, but her palms were sweating. And the closer they got to the ranch, the harder her heart beat.

Which was ridiculous. It wasn't like she had to face dear ol' dad once she got there. He was dead. Gone. Buried.

But his ghost would be there.

Not the see-through kind, of course. But she would

be staying in his house. She would be surrounded by his things. The ranch he built. The cattle and horses he raised. His personal possessions. Every waking minute she'd be bombarded by the stark evidence that he'd cared more for his ranch than he ever had for her or her mother.

She wasn't sure she was up to six months of that.

She plowed her fingers through her hair. She wanted to just walk away. But she couldn't do that to the Chads of the world. She knew the desperation people with major health problems and no insurance faced. So she'd spend the next six months facing her father's betrayal.

Even if it killed her.

She forced her mind from those ugly thoughts. Unfortunately, her mind jumped directly to the other new item in her life. McCade. Not a safer subject at all. The cowboy was too big, too…commanding.

Too damned sexy.

Oh, *man.* She ran her hands through her hair and drew in a big breath, trying to get enough oxygen into her system, trying to calm her nerves. But there wasn't enough air in the truck.

McCade looked over at her, his brows scrunched in concern. "You all right?"

"Oh yeah, peachy."

"Crissy, everything is going to be fine." His voice was quiet, encouraging.

But she didn't feel encouraged. She felt like her whole world was going to explode. Not only was Mc-

Cade making her feel things that had been safely in hibernation for the past three years, but anger and despair over her father's betrayal were already building in her like molten lava boiling beneath the earth's surface. And it boiled a little harder every time she thought of her father owning one of the biggest spreads in Texas. Every time she looked at the truck she was riding in.

Her father's truck.

It was big and fancy with every bell and whistle available. Leather upholstery, air-conditioning, extended cab and rear dual wheels. She shifted on the gray leather seat, feeling like she was betraying her mother's memory just by riding in the thing.

She tried to draw in another breath. Tried to ignore the anger simmering inside her. But she couldn't do it. She shook her head. "Do you have any idea how much medicine someone could buy for the cost of this gas-guzzling hog?"

McCade glanced over at her. "Are you thinking of how many Chads you can help if you sell it?"

"No, I'm thinking of my mother. She died of MS, did you know that?" She watched carefully for his reaction. She wanted to know if he'd known of her mother's plight. If he'd known she was sick and suffering and needed help while Warner had turned a blind eye and built his damned ranch.

Surprise and sympathy knitted his brow. "No, I didn't. I knew she was dead. That she'd died when she was only thirty-eight. So I assumed either disease or an accident had taken her. But I didn't know she had MS. I'm sorry. That's a tough disease."

She studied him, looking for any sign that he was dissembling. But his surprise seemed genuine. Which meant dear ol' dad had kept everything about her mother secret. Her state of poverty. Her disease. Her desperate requests for money.

Which helped explain McCade's loyalty to him.

She nodded her head. "MS is a tough disease. Especially when you don't have any money for hospital stays and doctors' appointments and drugs."

He looked over at her, concern etching his face. "She didn't have enough money to pay for her medical expenses?"

She laughed, a short, humorless sound. "Cowboy, there wasn't enough money to buy *food* half the time. And that was before she got sick. After…" Her words trailed off as old memories swamped her. Sad, desperate memories.

Memories of watching her mother go from a normal, healthy human being to someone who needed a cane to get around and then a wheelchair; finally she couldn't get around at all. Memories of standing over her bed and giving her aspirin after aspirin because they couldn't afford prescription painkillers. Memories of bone-deep desperation. And guilt.

God, the guilt.

Guilt that she hadn't been old enough to hold a job and take care of her mother. And then later, as she got older, guilt that the jobs she could get as a high school student and even later as a high school graduate only paid minimum wage. Not nearly enough to pay their bills, let alone have anything left over for doctors and medicine. Guilt that intensified even after her mother's death.

Why hadn't she thought of fund-raisers when her mother was alive? She'd helped countless families in the last few years collect money for medical crises. Why hadn't it occurred to her to do it for her own mother? Why had she been so damned helpless?

She swiped at the tear that suddenly spilled over her lashes and looked out the side window, hoping Mc-Cade hadn't noticed.

"I'm sorry it was so hard, Crissy. God, I'm sorry."

Great. He'd seen the tear. Well, tear or not, she wasn't helpless anymore. She shrugged and tipped her chin up. "I don't need your sympathy, Tex. It's been over for a long time."

He shook his head. "If your father had only known, I'm sure—"

"He knew." Her tone was as bitter as the anger simmering inside her. "I can't count the number of times my mother called him and asked—no begged—him to send us money."

Tate's head whipped around, his gaze flying to hers. Pure shock shone in those intense brown eyes.

"He never told you, did he? That he had a wife and daughter who needed his help?" She shook her head in disgust. "No, he wouldn't have. He wouldn't have wanted the people he worked with knowing what a scumball he was."

McCade shook his head, his expression intense. "Crissy, your dad didn't—"

She slashed her hand through the air. "Don't. Don't you *dare* defend my father to me or I'll get out of this truck and hike back to Alaska, I swear to God."

He drew a breath as if he would protest, even over her warning. But then he shut his mouth and turned his attention back to the road. His hands were wrapped so tightly around the steering wheel the knuckles were white. And a steady tick worked along his jaw.

He wasn't a happy camper.

Which made two of them. She peered through the windshield, looking for any sign of a big ranch ahead. Any sign they might be getting closer to their destination. But all she saw was the same thing she'd seen for the last million hours. Flat ground, scrub brush and a few low-lying hills. Lord, Texas must go on forever. "How much farther do we have to go?"

He tipped his head toward the hills that had been getting steadily closer for the last hour. "We're almost there. Those hills have a big valley in the middle of them. The ranch is nestled there."

Thank God. She wanted out of this truck.

As if sensing her climbing tension, he reached across the cab and gave her arm a reassuring squeeze. "Hang in there. Beginnings are always the hardest. Once we get you settled, it'll be easy riding."

She didn't believe that for a minute, but she soaked

up his brief touch, appreciating the support—ignoring the electric jolts of sexual energy.

A half mile down the road, he turned off onto a one-lane road that snaked toward the hills. And then it was only a matter of minutes before the truck wove around the middle hill and popped out into the valley.

Dear God, the place was enormous. There were buildings and corrals everywhere. It looked like a little city. She swallowed the bile rising in her throat. "Is all this my father's?"

McCade looked over at her, his gaze assessing. He obviously didn't want to upset her anymore. But after only a moment of hesitation, he gave his head a single, succinct nod.

Revulsion clogged her throat. Warner Trevarrow's own little empire.

McCade stopped the truck next to one of the big corrals and looked over at her. "Do you want me to give you a short tour, introduce you to some of the hands? Or do you want to go straight to your dad's house?" His voice was quiet now, gentle, much as his touch had been.

For the first time, she noticed the men wandering around. Many of them were glancing curiously at the truck. No doubt looking to see who the new owner was. She closed her eyes, blocking out their expectant faces. She couldn't meet them now. She couldn't possibly shake their hands and smile and pretend she was glad to be here. Or that the sight of this ranch did anything but turn her stomach. "Take me to the house." Her words were weak, shaky.

She felt the truck move again, winding this way and that. And then it slowed, stopped. "This is it."

She opened her eyes and looked out the windshield. In the day's waning light, a huge log house met her gaze. A three-story log house with high-pitched roofs, long balconies and lots of glass. Her stomach flipped again and an icy hand gripped her heart. The bastard. While she and her mother had been living in rat- and cockroach-infested rooms, the kind you paid for by the week, her father had been living in a luxury house. Damn his soul.

McCade's piercing brown eyes met hers. "Ready?"

She was never going to be ready. But she managed a mute nod.

With an encouraging smile, he got out of the truck, strode around to her side and opened the door.

Her brain said get out. But her limbs wouldn't move.

He took hold of her elbow, his big hand strong and warm as his fingers closed around her arm. "Come on, it's just a house."

It wasn't just a house. It was living proof of her father's betrayal. Living proof that he'd cared more for this cursed piece of land than he had for her mother. Or for her. The thought of spending one second inside its walls...

But there were too many Chads out there to wimp out now. She forced thoughts of her father from her mind, concentrated on the heat soaking into her from the cowboy's touch, and swung her legs out of the truck.

Once she was steady on her feet, he let go of her

arm, grabbed her bag from the small back seat and led the way up the walk.

She followed him, focusing on his broad shoulders, the ripple of muscle under his shirt, anything but the bile climbing up her throat.

At the house, McCade pushed the door open, stepped off to the side and waved her in.

She took a deep breath and stepped over the threshold.

The muted light of dusk filled the house, casting twilight and shadows everywhere.

McCade followed her in and flicked on the wall switch behind her.

Light flooded the room, bouncing off the polished wooden floors and illuminating the wide-open space. The room was huge, the ceilings here at the front of the chamber soaring the entire three stories. Combined with the giant windows lining the front wall, it almost seemed as if she were still outside.

She shook her head. What an egomaniacal show of grandeur.

She took in the round, open fireplace in the middle of the expanse with its tan textured rock and pounded black-iron fittings. Leather sofas and rock-back chairs surrounded it, making a conversation area. Other well-appointed sitting areas were arranged here and there around the big room as well. At the back of the room, a wide wooden staircase led to a balcony with several doors running along its back wall. Bedrooms, she presumed.

She looked to McCade, who'd moved into the room

and set her bag on one of the sofas by the fireplace. "Did anyone besides my father live here?"

He shook his head.

Of course. She strode across the floor toward a conversation area in the far corner of the room, right in front of the big windows.

McCade followed her. Not close enough to invade her space. But she could feel him behind her, letting her know she had his support. It was the only thing that kept her from howling with rage.

She stared at the leather sofa, the cowhide chair and the coffee table with its log legs and the giant slab of crosscut wood making up its surface. It was designed to look like some cowboy had gone out and made it in an afternoon, but the high-gloss shine and fancy wood grain told her it was an expensive piece. Damned expensive.

She raised her gaze to the wall behind the sofa. It was lined with tall mirrors, their shiny surfaces reflecting the room and the lights and her own sorry self. She stared at her reflection, then noticed how the ranch operation— its buildings, paddocks, fields and the low-lying hills that protected it all—stretched out behind her image.

She shook her head. How many times had her father stood here staring at his kingdom and his own vile reflection while she and her mother scrambled for food? While her mother lay dying of a disease that a little money could have gone a long way to alleviate. The arrogant bastard.

She drew a deep breath trying to calm her nerves,

trying to keep from screaming her rage at the cowboy standing behind her. A glass piece sitting on an end table caught her eye and she wandered over, letting the piece distract her. It was a beautiful color. Rich brown with golden streaks arcing through it.

It looked handblown, its free-flowing form reminiscent of a leaf floating from a tree. Very pretty. It reminded her of Dale Chihuly's work. One of the world's leading glass artists. She'd first seen his work when she was a waitperson for a caterer hosting one of his shows. After that, she'd made a point to catch his shows if she was in or near a town that was hosting one. She loved his work.

She picked the piece up, the smooth, heavy glass cool against her fingers. She and the other girls often ran auctions along with their fund-raising stunts as a way to boost the final money count. If this had been made by a local artist, maybe she'd talk him or her into donating a piece for the next event. She flipped the piece over, looking for a signature. The small black letters caught her eye immediately.

Chihuly.

Oh, God. She looked over at McCade, her anger boiling into fury. "Do you have any idea how much food or medicine I could have bought for this one piece of art?" She sure as hell could have paid a year's rent with it. And then she could have used her meager salary for medicine. She possibly could have bought her mother another year of life. The fury exploded. She sent the Chihuly sailing at the mirrors.

Glass crashed and rained down in brown and silver pieces.

McCade swore and came in low, hit her at the waist, scooped her over his shoulder and quickly carried her from the flying shards of glass.

She fought against his hold. "Put me down." There was a lamp over there she wanted to send into the next mirrored panel.

"Fine." He dumped her unceremoniously onto a sofa by the fireplace. "But I'm not going to let you tear the place up."

She bounced up immediately and tried to push past him.

He blocked her path easily with that big body of his.

Thirteen years of pain and frustration and helplessness roared through her. "Not your choice. Get out of my way, dammit." She shoved against him, and when he wouldn't move she started throwing punches.

He easily blocked anything that came near his face and merely kept her contained as the others rained harmlessly on his chest and arms.

Which just frustrated her more. She hit harder, quicker, pouring all her despair, all her anger into every punch. She felt tears pour down her cheeks, but she didn't stop to wipe them away. She just kept hitting. And hitting. And hitting. Until there was no more rage. No more energy. Nothing but despair.

She collapsed against his chest, the tears taking control. What was happening to her? Five minutes in this house and she was turning into her most despised object on earth. A helpless, crying female. But she couldn't stop the tears. Or the sobs that tore from her throat. She buried her face against his chest, trying to hide the waterworks, muffle the sounds.

He closed his arms around her, his body closing around hers like a warm, protective cocoon. "It's okay, I've got you."

But it wasn't okay. It wasn't okay at all. She'd promised herself at her mother's funeral she'd never be helpless again. But with her father's betrayal assaulting her from every angle, she felt helpless now.

McCade ran his hand over her back, soothing, comforting.

She absorbed his warmth and strength like the desert floor drinking in rain. It felt so good to have someone's arms around her. Felt good to feel like she wasn't absolutely alone in the world. She'd been alone for so, so long.

And he felt so damned good.

She snuggled closer, drinking in his heat, breathing in his spicy aftershave. It would be so easy to let him chase away the pain. But it wouldn't be smart. Not smart at all. Because if the electricity already building between them meant anything, she knew how they'd end up chasing the pain away. And she didn't want to go that way.

She was serious about her moratorium on men. She'd watched her mother try to find herself in men right up until the disease made it impossible. It had made a sad, lonely life for her mother. One Crissy had promised herself she'd never repeat. And just because she felt like her life was shattering around her now, it was no time to backslide.

She'd get through this next six months on her own. And then she'd return to her quest to discover who she was and what she wanted in life.

She pulled in one more long, deep breath of McCade's warm, musky scent, let him stroke her back one more time and then pulled herself from his arms.

Tate let her go, his arms suddenly cold and empty. She'd felt so right there. So damned right. He could have held her all night. Just held her.

A ruthless laugh echoed through his head. Yeah, right. He could have kept her in his arms all night, no problem. But holding would have turned into something much more active before long. And that was a trail he couldn't go down. Not with Crissy Albreit.

She already had enough complications in her life; she didn't need more. And sleeping with him was loaded with complications. So he let her go and promised himself he'd keep his comforting on a verbal level from now on. Safer for both of them. He watched her stride toward the sofa where he'd dumped her bag.

She swiped at the tears wetting her cheeks. "I'm sorry, I don't know what got into me. Hysterical, crying female isn't usually my style." Her voice was soft, embarrassed.

He didn't want her to be embarrassed. Didn't want her to think she had to hide her emotions from him.

"Don't be silly, you've had a trying twenty-four hours."

She hung her hands on her hips, staring at the mess her outburst had created. "God, you must think I'm a maniac."

"I think you're tired and sad and angry."

She expelled a long, shaky breath. "Yeah, I am. And with that in mind—" She picked up her bag. "I think I'll head upstairs. Those are the bedrooms up there, right?" She pointed to the doors lining the back balcony wall.

"Yep, take your pick."

She waved a hand toward the front door. "Come on, I'll walk you out."

"Go on to bed, I'll stay and clean up the glass."

She shook her head. "I clean up my own messes, Tex. I'll get it tomorrow morning. Now go on, I'm tired." She shooed him toward the door.

He strode across the wooden floors, his boots echoing in the cavernous room. He wasn't thrilled about the idea of leaving her alone all night. Not as upset as she was. But short of camping out on the living room sofa, something he was sure she'd be just tickled pink about, he didn't have much choice.

At the door's threshold he hesitated, looking back to her. "If you need anything, *anything,* my number is one on the speed dial. Don't be afraid to call, any time of the night. I'm a light sleeper and I'm right across the road."

She nodded, a faint smile turning her lips. "Got it. Good night."

He closed the door behind him and strode toward

the house he'd lived in for the last several years. The small log house that had been Warner's original homestead. Halfway there, he stopped and turned back to the big house. He imagined Crissy in the bedroom, unpacking her bag, getting ready for bed.

She'd looked tired, beat, when she'd closed the door on him. Like she was holding on to her poise by the barest of threads. And he suspected she was. With good cause. She believed her father had not only abandoned her and her mother, but hung them out to dry during their most desperate hours.

It was a belief he was going to have to straighten out. But it wasn't going to be easy. Or fun. Showing Crissy that the parent who'd raised her, the parent she'd obviously loved so dearly had been the one keeping them in poverty, the one who'd lied to her all these years, was going to take everything she believed to be true and shred it to pieces.

His gut clenched. He was good at shredding people's lives. But putting them back together? A cold sweat broke out on his palms. God knew, he hadn't been able to put his sister's life back together. He'd only taken a bad situation and made it worse. Far, far worse.

He clenched his fists and stared up at the stars appearing in the sky. "If there's a heaven up there, Warner, and you're in it, you damned well better be paying attention." His voice echoed fiercely as dusk faded to night. "I don't save damsels in distress, dammit. If you want me to tear this girl's life up, I expect you to be around to help put it back together."

Chapter Four

The next morning, Crissy flipped off the water in the fancy, glass-brick enclosed shower. After the last day and a half of extreme sports, mad travel and emotional turmoil, she was drained. She'd hoped a hot shower would revive her. But she still felt physically exhausted and emotionally bruised.

She stepped out of the tile-and-glass cubicle, the house's air-conditioning bringing goose bumps to her skin. She grabbed the towel hanging on the brass rack and started to towel herself dry, shaking her head at the ridiculously thick folds of terry cloth. The obvious wealth surrounding her made her angry and uncomfortable. She wanted out of this house. The need to run from its opulence had pushed at her all night long. But she didn't know where to go.

A walk had seemed like a good idea around midnight. But when she'd stepped out on the porch and discovered there were still a few cowboys strolling between the corrals, she'd retreated back into the house. She hadn't been up to facing more men like McCade. Men who were loyal to her father. Nor did she want to see them this morning.

She pulled on her panties and hooked her bra. She needed a day to regroup. A day to let the emotions swirling inside her settle before her head exploded and she did something she'd really regret. Like burn down this house and the rest of the ranch with it. She headed out of the bathroom into the adjoining bedroom.

The sound of male voices drifted through her closed door.

She stopped in her tracks, looking over toward the wooden portal. Was someone in the house?

No. Surely not.

But the voices certainly sounded like they were coming from downstairs. She quickly strode to the bed and pulled on the jeans and shirt she'd laid out.

The tinkle of broken glass filtered through the door.

Oh man, someone *was* in the house.

Forgoing shoes, she padded out of the room to the narrow balcony that ran in front of the upstairs rooms and peered over the railing.

Two cowboys were working diligently to clean up the mirror she'd shattered last night. One crouched low, holding a dustpan, while the other swept broken glass into it.

She didn't know the cowboy pushing the broom, but she recognized the broad back of the one holding the dustpan. "I thought I told you I clean up my own messes."

Both men looked up.

McCade straightened and turned to her, dustpan in hand. "And I would have let you, but then Braxton showed up and he's never been able to let a mess sit."

She shifted her gaze to the man standing behind McCade. He had neither McCade's height nor mass, but there was a bearing to him, a quiet confidence, that required neither to make his presence known. His six-foot frame was broad-shouldered, narrow-hipped and whipcord lean. The face that went with it, finely chiseled and, except for a scar arcing through one brow, classically handsome. She imagined he'd turned more than one cowgirl's head.

But she wasn't interested in his good looks. "And what were you doing in the house, Mr. Braxton? Did my father have an open-house policy? Anyone could wander in at will?" Despite her intention to keep her voice even, a bit of challenge sneaked in.

The man's expression turned sheepish. "My apologies. It wasn't my intention to disturb you. Your dad did have an open-door policy for the men who had regular business with him or needed access to the ranch's offices. I take care of the ranch's books." He waved a hand to the wall beneath the balcony. "I didn't stop to think you might want to change that policy." His Texas accent wasn't as deep as McCade's;

he was obviously not a native. But he'd been here awhile.

And she was no doubt stepping on his toes. *She* was the interloper here. The one who didn't belong. She plowed her fingers through her hair. "I won't be here long enough to change anything, Mr. Braxton. Feel free to go about your business. But, please, leave the mirror where it is. I'll put on some shoes and clean it up."

"Forget the mirror for now," McCade said. "You can clean it up later. I thought you might like an early morning ride. A little fresh air to clear your head. I brought a couple of horses over." He waved his hand toward the big picture window.

Sure enough, two horses were tied to the railing that ran along the wooden porch. A little frisson of excitement shot through her. Horses. A red one and a brown one with a black mane and tail. She'd always been fascinated by the creatures. And nothing sounded better than getting out of this house. "Okay, let's go for a ride. I'll clean up the mirror when I get back." She turned on her heel and hurried toward her room.

"Put something on with some kind of heel, Crissy. Not tennis shoes." McCade hollered after her.

She stared at the tennies next to the bed where she'd kicked them off last night, then switched her gaze to the small bag she'd brought to Alaska. She stuck her head back out the door. "All I have is tennies."

He made a face. "Okay, we'll make do for today. But you're going to need boots."

Like those were in her budget when she wouldn't be working for the next six months. She put her tennies on and skipped down the stairs to where the two cowboys stood talking. "Okay, let's go."

"All righty then." McCade smiled and headed for the door.

Braxton put out his hand just as she was about to stride past. "I just wanted to say welcome to the ranch, Miss Trevarrow. And offer my condolences for the loss of your father."

She tromped on the urge to tell the man she didn't need any condolences, but she wasn't up for that fight this morning. She shook his hand. "Thank you, Mr. Braxton, I appreciate the sentiment. But it's Albreit. Crissy Albreit." She followed McCade out the door, pulling it closed behind her.

As she strode over to where McCade was standing in front of the horses, she glanced inside the house.

Braxton was standing where they'd left him, his gazed fixed on the broom leaning against the wall by the shattered mirror.

She shook her head. "He's not going to leave that mirror for me to clean up, is he?"

McCade shrugged. "Probably not. Braxton has this thing about order. But a little cleanup won't kill him, so quit worrying about the mirror and pay attention to your horse. This is Sugar." He unwound the reins from the railing and backed the red horse up until she was standing out where Crissy had easy access to her.

She joined him at the horse's head, holding her

hand beneath the horse's nose. The mare's warm breath wafted over her skin, and then the horse dipped her head, nuzzling her. Crissy laughed. "She wants me to pet her."

McCade chuckled. "She's probably looking for a sugar cube, but she won't turn down a good rub." He stroked the mare's head, from the wide space between her eyes down to the soft nose nudging Crissy's hand, showing her what the mare might like.

Crissy followed his lead, stroking the mare, lingering at the muzzle. "It's like velvet here. Soft and warm."

McCade nodded. "It's one of my favorite spots, too."

She kept petting, admiring the mare's shiny red coat and her big, liquid brown eyes. Sugar leaned into her hand, obviously enjoying the attention. She laughed. "I like her, she's sweet."

"Yes, she is, but the day's a-wastin'. Let's get going. Have you ever ridden?"

She shook her head, excitement skittering through her. "Always wanted to, but there was never time or money."

"Well, there's plenty of time now and it's not going to cost you a dime." He draped the reins over the horse's neck, took hold of Crissy's elbow and guided her back toward the saddle.

In short order, he had her on top of the horse, the reins securely tucked into her left hand. Now if she could just reach the stirrups.

McCade smiled. "Hang in there for a sec, we'll get those shortened right up." He gently pulled against her knee, moving her leg back. "For future reference, there's a buckle here, under this flap, where you can adjust their length." He reached near the top of the saddle, his hands gently bumping against her thigh.

Heat shot through her. She stared down at his hands. Great hands. Big, strong, competent. She imagined them touching her, just about where they were now.

Oh, man.

As if sensing her thoughts, McCade looked up. Desire flared in his eyes. But he quickly hid it, looking back to the buckle and making quick work of the task at hand. He stepped back, breaking the contact, and nodded toward the stirrup. "Try that." There was a telltale roughness in his voice.

She slid her foot into the wide, wooden cup, ignoring the electric tingles shooting through her. With her world in complete chaos, now was the worst possible time to let a man's touch distract her. "That's—" Lordy, her voice carried the same roughness his had. She cleared her throat. "That's better."

"Good." He took another step back. "Why don't I let you get the other one."

Good idea. It took a little longer with her working the buckles, but it wasn't long before she had the other stirrup shortened up. "Okay, now what?"

Already settled on his own horse, he gave her a

quick lesson in how to make the horse go, turn and stop. "Any questions?"

She shook her head, anxious to be off.

"Then let's go." He nudged his horse with his heel.

She copied his actions, bumping her horse. Sugar moved obediently forward, falling in beside McCade's horse. She was riding a horse! Actually telling it what to do. Cool.

She moved her rein hand to the right, letting the leather strap pull gently on Sugar's neck. The horse veered to the right. Crissy moved her hand to the left. Sugar moved nimbly back beside McCade. She smiled. "Power steering. Very cool."

McCade smiled back. "Isn't it, though."

"Where are we going?"

"Thought we'd ride out to Pillar Creek. It's one of the prettiest places on the ranch. And since we moved the cattle off it last week, it'll be quiet."

"Pillar Creek sounds perfect." After the last twenty-four hours, quiet sounded good. Being out away from everything and everyone sounded good. Especially since every hand wandering around the paddock was checking her out. And no wonder. She held their future in her hands.

A cold sweat broke out on her palms. What would they think if they knew she was planning on selling the place? Or maybe burning it to the ground? What would they think if they knew how she felt about Warner Trevarrow?

She might find a few who didn't like the man any

better than she did. It was a big ranch. Any job she'd ever worked at had disgruntled employees. But she suspected most of them would be like McCade.

Braxton certainly had been. His condolence had been genuine. She'd seen the respect he'd felt for her father in his expression. A ranch full of little Warner worshippers could make her life here very uncomfortable.

She did her best to smile back at the men watching her as she and McCade made their way through the paddocks. But she didn't speak to any of them. She wasn't brave enough. Not yet. So she took the coward's way out, silently following McCade out of the paddock area.

As they got farther from the buildings, she began to relax and enjoy the view around her. It was midspring, the grass that had wintered over was knee-high and brown, but everything was greening up near the ground, where new shoots were sprouting. It was pretty, the long, dried grass swaying softly in the early morning breeze. And the scenery directly in front of her...

She smiled, studying McCade. His shirt pulled tight across his shoulders, accenting their broadness and defining the hard muscles of his arms and back. His long, strong legs stretched easily to his stirrups. His lean hips rocked gently with the horse's motions. Man, oh man. Was there anything sexier than a cowboy in the saddle?

Not on this planet. And with each step they took

away from the ranch, she became more aware of that insidious little fact. More aware of the man in front of her. His quiet strength and the sexual tension that crackled around him like heat lightning gathering for a storm. She shook her head. No doubt about it, the devil had his tempt-the-sex-starved-woman down to a fine, fine art.

She closed her eyes, struggling to block out the images of McCade streaming through her head. Images of those lean hips rocking against her. But it wasn't easy, and as they got farther and farther from the ranch, closer and closer to the moment when they would slip around the base of the hill and find themselves alone, the thought got harder and harder to control. Maybe coming on this ride hadn't been such a good idea, after all.

She peeked over her shoulder, gazing back at the ranch. The men working in and around the corrals were still visible. She looked over to her father's house, its giant glass windows glinting richly in the early morning rays, shouting money and power and brutal betrayal. Nothing but tortuous reminders for her there.

She looked back to the man riding in front of her, her thigh tingling where his hands had touched her earlier. Another sort of torture altogether.

She gritted her teeth. It was going to be a long, long six months.

Tate rode quietly beside Crissy. They were in open country now. The morning was quickly warming up as the sun rose steadily above the horizon.

Crissy was doing well with the horse, her touch smooth and gentle. A rarity in a greenhorn, but not totally unexpected. After all, the Alpine Angels made big bucks for their fund-raisers because they were athletically inclined and could pull off even the most extreme sports. Sitting on a horse was a cakewalk compared to most of the things Crissy did. Particularly since they'd done nothing more strenuous than walk.

He cast another glance her way. She'd been strung as tight as barbed wire when they first left the house, but the land was working on her, slowly getting her to relax. That was one of the reasons he'd brought her out here. There was nothing like fresh air and open country to soothe the soul.

He wished it would do a little more to soothe the sexual tension singing between them, but it didn't seem to be helping in that area at all. In fact, the solitude just made it worse. So when he looked at Crissy, he did his best not to let his gaze dawdle in places that would only tighten the fit of his jeans. And he did his best not to react when her gaze skated over him, lingering in places that made his blood run hot and his pulse kick into overdrive.

He guided his horse, Cutter, to a small outcropping of rocks, a natural high spot that looked down over the land before them. Reining the gelding in, he pointed to the lazy winding creek that serpentined through the flat lands. "Pillar Creek."

Crissy sidled Sugar up next to him, gazing at the panorama. "Pretty. Good choice, Tex."

"I thought you'd like it. It's one my favorites. Was one of your dad's, too."

She grimaced. "Can we not talk about him today?"

His gut clenched. The pleasant ride was over. "Unfortunately, we need to talk about him. Him and your mom."

Her gaze snapped back to him, her lips pressed into a thin, hard line. "You jerk. You didn't bring me out here for fresh air. You brought me out here to ambush me."

"I brought you out here because I thought you might enjoy some fresh air while we talked."

She snorted at his excuse.

He sighed. "Fine. I ambushed you. But, this is a mountain we have to get over. And it's been my experience that when you're facing something unpleasant, sooner is better than later."

She turned her horse away from him. "Not today it isn't."

He nudged Cutter into motion, easily regaining his place beside Sugar. "Running away won't make the problem disappear."

She shot him a black scowl. "No. But it might make you disappear." She turned Sugar away from him again and nudged the old mare with her heels.

Sugar picked up her pace, but didn't budge from a walk.

He effortlessly dropped in beside her again. "Sugar's the oldest horse we still put a saddle on here at the Big T, Crissy. She's twenty-six. Takes more than a nudge to get her out of a walk. Takes a good, hard kick."

"Twenty-six?" Frustration crumpled her brow. "And even if I managed to get her out of a walk, you wouldn't have any trouble keeping up. Would you?" She scowled at the animal beneath him.

"Not a bit. Cutter here is still in his prime."

She huffed in disgust. "And you want to pretend this isn't an ambush?"

"An ambush is used when you want to take something from someone or hurt them. I don't want to do either. But we have some hard things to talk about, and I need you to stay around while we do. So yes, I stacked the deck in my favor. Shoot me."

"Careful, cowboy. I don't have a gun on me, but I'm sure dear old dad, good Texan that he no doubt was, has a roomful of them at home."

Note to himself: remove all ammunition from the house while she's putting Sugar away. "I'll deal with that when we get there. Until then—"

"I told you yesterday I didn't want you trying to justify my father to me. I haven't changed my mind."

"I'm not going to justify anyone to you. I'm simply going to relate the story your father told me about what happened twenty-two years ago. What you want to do with that information is up to you."

"I already know what happened. On a dark, rainy night, my father kicked my mother and me out of his house and told her he never wanted to see us again."

"Correction, your father kicked your *mother* out, he never intended she should take you with her. And—"

"And you think that's okay? A man kicking his wife

out of their house in the middle of the night with nothing but the clothes on her back?" Outrage sounded in her voice.

Outrage she had every right to feel. "No, I don't. It was a bad decision. One made in a drunken rage. One your father regretted every day of his life from that night forward."

"Oh, please. If the man regretted his actions, he had plenty of opportunity to make up for them. Do you have any idea how many times my mother called him, asking for help?"

This was the lie at the center of Crissy's anger for her father. The misconception he had to break. The misconception that was going to send her world spinning. He braced himself for the fight and shook his head. "She never called, Crissy. That's what I was trying to tell you in the truck yesterday when you cut me off. After your mother took you that night and left, your father never heard from her again."

"That's a lie. *She called.* Time and time again, asking for money. Asking for help. And Warner Trevarrow always told her to get lost."

"Were you ever in the room when she called? Did you ever *hear* the calls? Or did she just tell you about them?"

"Of course I heard them." Righteous indignation sounded in her voice.

But he suspected she'd answered more out of anger and reflex than truth. "Are you sure? Think hard."

She sent him another fuming stare, but he could see the doubt sweeping into her thoughts.

He let her ponder a bit, praying her mother hadn't put on some charade where she'd talked into a phone with God knew whom or what on the other end, making her daughter think she was talking to her dad. It would be a harder lie to combat. Not that he couldn't combat it. But he'd like to use as small a hammer as possible.

He sat quietly in the saddle, the sound of rustling grass and the soft creak of leather wafting on the warming breeze. A hawk's lonely cry drifted down from the clear blue sky. He glanced up, spotting the majestic bird gliding playfully on the thermals overhead.

Crissy followed his gaze, spotting the bird immediately. She smiled, a smile that momentarily erased the shadows from her eyes.

The hawk suddenly dove toward the ground, his beak leading the way, his wings tucked tight against his body. Just before reaching the grass, he flared his wings and reached forward with his feet. A split second later he was winging toward the sky again, a mouse dangling helplessly from deadly claws.

Crissy lowered her gaze to his, the shadows flitting back into her eyes. "It's never quite as idyllic as we want to believe, is it?"

He shook his head. "No."

She exhaled a long sigh. "I don't actually remember if I heard any of my mother's calls or not. But that doesn't mean I didn't. My mother died seven years ago, and we'd given up on my father coming to our aid a couple years before that. It was a long time ago. But what could possibly have been the point of her lying to me? She needed help. *Desperately. We* needed help. Why *wouldn't* she have called?"

"I don't know. But from what your dad told me, your mom had issues. Ones your dad said kept her from thinking rationally sometimes."

Pain and anger slashed across her face. "She might have had 'issues.' And she might not have always thought 'rationally,' but she wasn't delusional, for pity's sake. She was together enough that she *never* turned her back on her little girl. Unlike the man you're trying to paint as a bloody saint."

"I'm not trying to paint anyone as a saint. Least of all your father. God knows, he'd turn over in his grave if he thought I was. I'm just trying to tell his side of the story."

"Then tell it. But don't expect me to believe every word out of your mouth."

"All I'm asking is that you listen with an open mind."

"Fine, my mind is open."

If the underlying anger in her words was any indication, her mind wasn't very open. But since it was likely all he'd get, he'd best get to it. "Did your mother ever tell you why he threw her off the ranch?"

Her lips twisted in disgust. "Said he found someone new. Someone younger, prettier. Someone without a toddler to take care of." Pain sounded in her words as she voiced her belief that her father didn't want her.

He locked his gaze on hers. "Your father never considered you anything but the most wonderful of gifts, Crissy. *Never.*"

Tears gathered in her eyes. "How would you know? You weren't—"

"No, I wasn't there. But I know because I saw the pain and longing in your dad's eyes every time he spoke of you. Heard the pride in his voice when he'd tell one of the memories he had of you. Memories that were old and few, but more precious to him than anything in this world."

More moisture filled her eyes, but she didn't let the tears fall. She might want to believe her father had missed her. But the anger underneath those tears told him she didn't. Not yet. And it would take a lot more talking on Tate's part before she'd even consider opening her mind. "It wasn't your father who found someone new, Crissy. It was your mother."

"Oh, come on, you can come up with something more original than just flipping the story around, can't you?"

"Yeah, I probably could if I was making it up. But I'm not making it up. I'm going to tell you exactly what your father told me. No embellishments to make your father sound more innocent. No assumptions about what I think anyone was thinking that night. You'll have to decide for yourself what you want to believe and what you don't."

"Fine. So my mother found someone new. Who was that?" Pure sarcasm sounded in her voice.

"I don't know his name. He was a drifter, apparently. A cowboy who'd come through for the roundup."

"That's convenient for the story."

He ignored the comment and pushed on. "It was a Saturday night and your father had let half the hands go early so they could enjoy themselves while he worked late with the other half. When he finally got home, he found you in your crib, Rosa, the housekeeper, watching you, and your mother gone. When he asked Rosa where your mother was, she said she'd headed to town with the first wave of cowboys. He wasn't worried at first, too worried, anyway. It wasn't the first time your mother had gotten impatient with him for being late and headed into town early to drink and dance with the ranch hands."

Her lips pressed into a thin line.

Did that mean she recognized the behavior? And didn't approve? Warner had said Vera was a big party girl. That she craved attention. Especially male attention. There was no reason that would have changed after she left Warner. In fact, it very possibly could have gotten worse.

But speculating about what Crissy was thinking wouldn't get him anywhere. "When he got to the bar, your mom wasn't there. Just a bunch of cowboys doing their best to avoid your dad. When he finally pinned one down, the man reluctantly told him your mom had left with one of the new guys. Supposedly just to check out a bar farther down the street, one that played pop music instead of country."

Crissy raised her chin in defense. "Maybe they did. My mom never did like country."

"No, your dad said she didn't. But as much as he wanted to believe the two had left simply for the music, he didn't. And he didn't think the other cowboys believed it, either. But, since your mom had told the hands she and the drifter would be back after a quick dance or two, and since your dad didn't want anyone to know he doubted her, he sat down, pretended everything was fine—and started drinking."

She rolled her eyes. "Now there's the perfect solution. Why didn't he just go looking for her?"

"Eventually he did. But he didn't find them at the bar down the street. He found them at the hotel at the edge of town."

She closed her eyes, pain and sadness washing across her features. "Oh, Mom. What were you thinking?"

The words were whispered so softly he barely heard them. But he heard. Had her mother brought an endless string of men home? Had she left a young girl home alone while she went man-hopping?

But however sad or dark the memories were, Crissy didn't let them suck her down. With a determined shake of her head, she pulled her shoulders back and opened her eyes to meet his gaze. "Okay, so my mother made a mistake. A big one. But you're not going to convince me it was okay for dear ol' Dad to throw her out on the street and tell her to get lost because of it. He wants to divorce her. Fine. But they had a kid together. He owed her child support, dammit."

She shifted in the saddle. "Do you have any idea how my mother had to compromise her living standards because she had to support me all by herself? She didn't have any skills. How the hell did Dad think she was going to put a roof over our heads? Food in our stomachs? And later, when she got sick. How did he think she was going to pay for her medical expenses when she had to feed and clothe me?"

A silent string of words cowboys didn't repeat in front of women pounded through his head. Not only had Crissy had to endure the hardships of poverty, but she blamed her very existence for putting her mother in that ugly situation. Dammit, dammit, *dammit*.

But he couldn't back down now. "No one knew better than your father that he made a mistake that night. Unfortunately, he didn't confront your mother at the hotel, when he was only half-drunk. At that point, maybe he would have been thinking clearly enough to make a better decision. But he drove home instead and proceeded to get rip-roaring drunk.

"By the time your mom wandered home, he was completely out of control. The second she walked through the door, he told her to pack her bags and get out. Told her he didn't ever want to see her again. Then he stormed into his study, locked the door and drank until he passed out."

Crissy looked at him with disbelief and outrage. "And what? He expected her to go and leave her child behind? He thought a mother would walk away from her child because some drunken cowboy told her to leave?"

"I think it's fair to say with a bottle of Jack Daniel's in his system, he probably wasn't thinking beyond his wounded pride or the pain he felt at your mother's betrayal, period."

Her lips thinned into a hard line. But she didn't say anything.

"When your dad came to the next morning, he realized that as mad as he was at your mom he didn't want her to leave. He'd known when he married her she'd had emotional issues. He'd wanted to work it out with her. But when he went looking for her, hoping she'd ignored his drunken tirade and stayed, he realized not only had she left, she'd taken you with her. Desperate to find you both, he raced to town hoping to track you down at one of the local hotels. Or at the bus station."

"But we were already gone." Her words were whisper soft.

He nodded. "A man at the barber shop had seen your mother hitching a ride out of town with a couple who'd stopped at the gas station. The man didn't know the car or the couple in it. He thought it was probably a couple just passing through on their way to who knew where."

"Okay, so you have a story that suggests my mom was the one who played around on my dad instead of the other way around. That hardly proves my mom never called my dad after they split up. It doesn't prove he didn't refuse to take my mom's calls."

"No, it doesn't. But now that you know your dad's story, I think these will convince you." He pulled Cutter to a stop, reached into his saddlebag, pulled out the papers he'd put in there earlier and held them out to her.

She stopped Sugar, staring at the papers, suspicion and trepidation clouding her expression. "What are those?"

"Read them and find out."

She looked at the papers as if they might turn into a snake and bite her. But then, determination straightening her spine, she snatched the papers from his hand and gave the top one a quick read. "So, it's some private investigator's bill made out to my father. So what?"

"It's a private investigator's bill from the search your father started the day you and your mother left. A search to find you both."

She looked back at the bill, studying it more carefully. "Even if my father did look for my mother in the beginning, that doesn't mean he didn't change his mind later. My mother told me she didn't try to contact him until I was about five. By then, Daddy dear might have decided he had better things to spend his money on. Like this ranch," she said pointedly.

"Look at the dates, Crissy."

Her gaze moved to the top of the page.

"You'll notice the top one is from twenty-two years ago. The month after you and your mother disappeared, to be exact. The second one is from five years later. The third five years after that. And the last one is from last month."

She flipped through the pages, verifying the dates. But when she looked up there was nothing but stubbornness on her face. "Four bills over twenty-two years doesn't constitute any great search. So his conscience kicked into gear now and then. That doesn't mean it was in working order when my mother called for help."

"God, you're tough."

"You bet I am. Watching my mom struggle to keep a roof over our heads and food in our bellies when I was young, and taking over those chores after my mom got sick, made me that way."

Yes, it would have. And while he admired the loyalty that made her cling to the belief that her mother had called, that her mother had done everything possible to provide for her daughter, he couldn't let her go on believing it. "I brought only four bills out this morning, but there's a stack of them a foot high in your father's office. Bills from every month for those twenty-two years. I'll show them to you when we get back if you need more proof."

"I don't want to see them," she snapped.

No, he didn't imagine she did. But... "Sooner or later, you're going to have to admit your mother wasn't telling you the whole truth. That your mother might have been responsible for keeping you in such poverty and misery."

Panic filled her expression. Panic and anger and...pain. Tears pooled in her eyes. "Why would she do that? What possible reason could she have to keep my father out of our lives, to withhold medical attention for herself?"

"I don't know. Like you've pointed out on several occasions, I didn't know your mom. But you did. Can you think of any reason why she wanted to keep your dad out of your lives? Because it seems pretty obvious to me that she did. Why else would she change her name from Trevarrow to Albreit if she wasn't trying to hide from him?"

"Oh, come on, the change of name doesn't prove anything. Women change their names when their marriages don't work out all the time."

"Back to their maiden names, yes. Or they marry again and take the name of their new spouse. Sometimes women will even take the name of an old spouse, but Albreit isn't any of those things."

A little more panic crawled into Crissy's expression. "No, it isn't."

"Do you have another explanation for the name change?"

She shook her head, confusion and frustration taking over her face. "Until yesterday I would have told you my mother did it to protect me."

"Protect you from what?"

She grimaced. "Hearing from my own father's lips that he didn't want anything to do with us."

He gave her a questioning look.

"When I first found my mom's marriage certificate and my birth certificate after her death, discovered that my last name hadn't been Albreit, I thought she must have realized early on that eventually I'd get old enough to look up my father. So, she'd changed our name to make sure I never found him. That way she could control whether I contacted him or not. Control whether or not I had to hear him tell us he didn't want anything to do with us."

"And now what do you think?"

She looked into the distance, her expression getting bleaker by the moment. "Now, I don't know what to think."

Great, he'd taken a life he suspected had been difficult on the best of days and removed the one pin of stability from it. Now he had to see where the pieces fell.

And pray to God he could put them back together before she decided jumping out of another plane or some other deadly stunt was a better way to spend her time. Because he suspected the Angels' penchant for extreme sports was as much about four troubled young women pushing back at an unfair world as it was about making money for those in need. And that was a dangerous path he didn't want Warner's daughter traveling down.

Chapter Five

Crissy sat outside her bedroom on the balcony that ran the length of the back of the house, its railing facing the hill she and McCade had ridden around to get to Pillar Creek this morning. She'd wandered out because she'd needed some fresh air. And because while the front side of the house faced the busy portion of the ranch, the back faced nothing but the Texas countryside. It was quiet here.

Quiet.

Still.

Peaceful.

After the day she'd had she needed that. Desperately.

She rocked gently in one of the Texas-sized rockers that were strewn around the balcony and drew in a deep breath, trying to calm her ratcheting nerves as she leaned back, propped her feet up on the railing and watched the sun dip beneath the hill's top. The already waning twilight faded to night. Staring at the twinkling stars, she let the day's emotions take hold of her.

Fresh tears pooled in her eyes. Tears she'd been fighting all day. Tears of frustration and sadness and anger. After McCade's little bombshell on the trail, she'd come back to the ranch and spent the day sifting through the bills in her father's office. It had made for a tumultuous afternoon.

Footsteps echoed in the dark.

She quickly swiped at the tears and glanced toward the edge of the house where the sound of crunching gravel reverberated through the night. Who was wandering back here? The sound of crunching gravel turned into that of someone climbing the stairs at the end of the balcony. McCade's head appeared as he made his way up the steps, the moonlight glinting off the sharp angles and planes of his face.

She looked heavenward, praying for strength. "Tex, I'm not sure I'm up for another one of your surprises. Seems like every time you appear on the horizon, my world gets a little shakier."

He stepped onto the balcony and held up his hands, a bottle in one, two shot glasses in the other. "No surprises. Just thought a good stiff drink would go down good about now."

"A little anesthetic for the havoc you created earlier?"

He winced, striding over to her and setting the bottle and glasses on the rail. "Something like that."

She drew a deep breath, feeling guilty for dumping her bad mood on him. "Sorry. I'm shooting the messenger, I know. But, unfortunately, the two people I want to be raking over the coals right now aren't here. And—"

"I am." He extracted a lime and small knife from his shirt pocket and set them on the railing.

She nodded.

He removed a saltshaker from his front jeans pocket and put it next to the lime. "That's okay. I can take it."

Yes, he seemed to have as much inner strength as outer strength. He absorbed all the anger she threw his way with the calm acceptance of a man who had a bone-deep understanding of the world around him and where he belonged in it. And because she had never known where she belonged in this world, it was a quality that made him just that much more appealing.

Too damned appealing. Squelching those thoughts, she concentrated on the bottle in his hand. Tequila. Of course. The lime and salt should have given it away. But her brain wasn't overly functional at the moment.

He poured two shots and handed her one. "Salt and lime?"

"Absolutely." She curled her free hand into a soft fist, licked the top finger near the big knuckle and held it out.

McCade shook the saltshaker over it and handed her a wedge of lime.

She waited while he got his own drink ready, then held her glass up in toast. "To a quiet, *uneventful* day tomorrow."

"Hear! Hear!" He clinked his shot glass to hers.

They both licked the salt from their hands, downed their shots and bit into their limes.

The liquor rocketed down her throat, hit her stomach and raced into her bloodstream. She rocked back, closing her eyes, letting the warmth slide through her. Letting the alcohol relax the muscles along the back of her neck, the tight knot in her stomach and chest.

Something clinked against the lip of her glass. She opened her eyes to find McCade pouring her another shot. "Easy, I'm not much of drinker."

"Just sip at this one." He set the bottle down, grabbed the saltshaker and held it up.

She held her hand out.

He sprinkled more salt and cut her another slice of lime. Then he proceeded to pour himself another shot and downed it without the salt and lime embellishments.

She raised a brow. Had this day been as unpleasant for him as it had for her? Maybe. While she'd been certain from the moment she'd met him that he was determined to do whatever was required to fulfill his obligation to her father, including playing dirty, she didn't think he liked making her unhappy.

She touched the end of her tongue to the salt on her hand and took a tiny sip of tequila as he filled his shot glass again. He obviously planned to stay awhile. "You going to pull up a rocker or just tower over me while we drink?"

He pulled one of the other rockers alongside hers, grabbed his drink, sat and propped his feet next to hers on the railing. "Pretty out here tonight."

She stared at the full moon hanging over the distant hills. "I will give dear ol' Dad that. He picked a beautiful place to build his little empire."

McCade winced but he didn't say anything. He just sat, quietly rocking, occasionally sipping at his drink, his shirt gently brushing her arm as his chair moved slowly back and forth, his heat seeping into her shoulder like a warm, tantalizing breeze.

Her traitorous gaze slid to his dusty cowboy boots, ran up his long, denim-clad legs and settled at the masculine bulge at the top of those legs. Oh, man. She dragged her eyes off him and took another fortifying swallow of tequila.

McCade took a sip of his own drink, then turned his gaze on her. "You want to talk about the ranch? Or your dad? You must have a million questions."

He was back to pushing again. She slanted him a look. "What if I say no?"

"Then we'll just sit here, watch the moon climb up the sky."

She laughed. "And how long do you think you'll be able to do that before you break down and bring the subject up again?"

He smiled, rocking gently in his chair. "Maybe a minute or two."

"If I'm lucky." Her thoughts slid back to the troubling questions that had plagued her all afternoon. "My mom was raised in group and foster homes, did you know that?"

He looked over at her, the moon's silvery light highlighting and shadowing his face. "I didn't know."

"Her parents were killed in an automobile accident when she was eight." She closed her eyes, thinking how tiny, how vulnerable a little girl of eight was. "Her father and mother didn't have any family that could take her in. So my mother became a ward of the state."

"And she was never adopted?"

"Nope. She used to dream of it. Said once she recovered from her parents' deaths, she'd lay awake nights and fantasize about a couple coming along and falling in love with her, adopting her and bringing her home. More than anything else in the world, she wanted a home and someone to love her."

"But it didn't happen?"

"No. And it left a hole in her, I think. Made her desperate for someone's love. Which is what I don't understand. If my father loved her, why'd she play around on him?"

He shrugged philosophically. "The Big T was a new ranch then; your father was just starting to build it. If she was needy for attention, maybe he didn't have enough time for her. Maybe she felt neglected."

She thought of all the men who'd come and gone in her mother's life. "Maybe. God knows, when Mom was with a man she wanted all his attention. *Needed* all his attention. She even hated it when they went to work. I think it's why most of the guys left. They knew whatever they gave would never be enough."

"So you're at least entertaining the thought your mother might have contributed to what happened all those years ago."

"I'm entertaining the idea. But I still have reservations."

He watched her, his gaze concerned and sympathetic. "What's bothering you the most?"

"If my mom never intended to ask for my dad's help, why did she pretend to call? Why tell me she was *going* to call?"

"I don't know. Maybe just to make your dad look bad. It wouldn't be the first time one spouse vilified another."

"Maybe." But that answer didn't ease the turmoil roiling inside her.

"Is it that she pretended to call that bothers you, or that she so obviously didn't want help from your dad?"

"The latter, I think. It just seems so…self-destructive." She thought back, the faces of several men flashing through her head. Men that had been involved with her mother, sometimes for months. She sighed, dropping her head back against the rocker. "But now that I think about it, self-destructive is a pretty good way to describe Mom's relationships. Most of the men she brought home were users. Takers. And once there was no more to take, they left."

"Did she ever see any of them again? After they left? Try to rekindle the relationship?"

Now there was a provoking bunch of questions. "No, she didn't. As much as my mother wanted to be loved. As much as she wanted a man to come into her life and stay, if things didn't work out, it was over. Completely over. Once they left our house or we left theirs, she never saw them again. Not to settle up on old bills or for a cup of coffee or for anything."

"She *never* saw them again?" Surprise sounded in his voice.

"Never." She stared up at the stars, trying to make sense out of that quirk. Trying to understand why her mother hadn't ever called her father. And why she'd gone to such lengths to make sure Crissy never did, either. "Maybe she felt like too much of a loser after a relationship failed and she just wanted to put it behind her, pretend it never happened. Or maybe, after being tossed from one foster family to the next as a kid, she thought further contact was futile. Whatever the reason, I never saw any of them again. In fact, we usually moved to a different town after a breakup. Although that could just as well have had to do with her trying to make sure my father never found us."

"You've been thinking about the name change thing?"

She nodded. "When you put all the pieces together, it certainly looks like she was making sure he didn't find us. Maybe she was afraid he'd take me away. Maybe… I don't know." Her brain was too numb to think anymore.

"You have to realize that with her gone, you may never understand her motivations for everything she did."

Sadness washed through her. "I know."

"It sounds like you moved around a lot. Did you like it? Seeing new places?" Having forced her to face some of the hard truths of her past, he changed the subject, steering her on to easier ground.

And she was glad for it. "I hated it. Mom wasn't the only one who dreamed about having a house. A home. Before she got sick, even after sometimes, Mom and I used to talk about having our own house."

She smiled thinking of those times. "We'd plan it all out, you know? First we'd decide what kind it was. A one-story ranch or a two-story contemporary or just a little grandma house on a quiet corner. Then we'd decorate it. Plan what kind of curtains we'd have in the kitchen. And where we'd put the garden. We always planned a garden. With red roses and pansies."

"Just roses and pansies?"

She nodded, laughing. "Well, we wanted more than a few of them. My mom loved pansies. Not all of them, but the purple and yellow ones. She wanted a whole sea of them. And—"

"You wanted roses."

"Yes. Red roses, mind you. They had to be red." She smiled, remembering. "It was fun, planning. Dreaming."

"But you never had a house of your own?" His smooth southern drawl wafted through the warm night air.

And over her like silk on water. She closed her

eyes against the tantalizing sensation and concentrated on the subject at hand. "Are you kidding? There were times when we couldn't even afford a cheap hotel. There was one time, though, when Mom was dating this guy with money. Not money like this." She waved her hand, indicating the Big T. "But enough money he could help pay the rent and have a little left over for a few fun things. An ice-cream cone from Dairy Queen. A movie on Saturday night. Anyway, Mom and I bought some material and hand stitched some kitchen curtains for the tiny apartment we were renting at the time. That was cool."

"Sounds…cool."

She shot him a sideways glance. "You don't think it sounds cool. You think it sounds pitiful."

"Not pitiful. But…hard."

She shrugged. "It was sometimes. But I had my mom. I always knew she loved me."

"Your father loved you, too." He locked his gaze on hers. "And he was looking for you, Crissy. He—was—looking."

A million emotions pounded through her. Pain, frustration, loss. "Yes, it looks like he was. And I'm softening toward him. But I'd be lying if I said I didn't feel guilty about it."

"That's understandable, if not exactly fair. You've thought negatively about your father for twenty-two years; that isn't going to change overnight. Particularly since your father's version of what happened that night isn't any prettier than your mother's."

"No, it's not." Her voice was as weary as she felt.

"But...I would suggest you think very hard about cutting your dad out of your life just because your mom did. You need to find a way to let them both into your heart." He stood, pulled a small envelope from his back pocket and handed it to her. "Your dad left this for you. I don't know what's in there. But maybe it will help." He stood and headed for the end of the balcony.

She stared at the envelope, then at his retreating back. The need to call him back danced on her tongue. She didn't want to be alone. It seemed as if she'd faced every scary moment of her life alone. She didn't want to face this one that way, too.

Unfortunately, she was afraid to think where her current vulnerability coupled with the sexual tension between them might lead if her father's missive upset her and McCade decided to hold her again. McCade might have the wherewithal to keep things in check, to keep things at a comforting level, but she was pretty sure she didn't. So she clamped her mouth shut and watched him walk away.

Just before he headed down the stairs, he stopped and turned to her. "You said you've always wanted a home. This could be your home, Crissy. It's a beautiful place. A good place."

Old longing rushed in, but only for a moment. She shook her head. "I don't think so, Tex. My mother's memory aside, this place is too rich for my taste. I could never own anything this lavish. There are too many people out there doing without."

He shrugged. "So downsize. Or make the place work for you. Your dad plowed the money the ranch made back into the place so he'd have something grand to bring you and your mom back to if he found you. But you don't have to do the same. Stop growing the place and use the money for your charity. Or whatever else you'd like to use it for."

The idea slid through her, sneaking underneath her confusion and pain to tease her, tempt her. She liked the idea of having a steady income to use for her charity. But…could she make enough peace with the past to make this her home?

"Just something to think about," he pointed out.

She shot him a wry smile. "Like I need more of that."

He returned the smile. "I'll see you tomorrow." Without another word, he disappeared down the stairs.

She looked at the envelope clutched in her hand.

A card.

From her father.

Mouth dry, heart pounding, she broke the seal and pulled the card out with shaking fingers. Opening it, she angled her body so the small amount of light coming from her bedroom fell on the card, highlighting the boldly scrawled words. Holding her breath, she read.

Crissy,

I've composed a dozen notes. All of them from my heart, but most of them were long-winded and did more to appease my conscience than anything else. Now I've decided to say only the things that matter.

I've missed you—more than I can ever tell.

I love you—more than you will ever know.

I'll be watching from above, or perhaps below, doing what I couldn't in life—taking care of you.

Love,

Dad

She closed her eyes against the words. Words she would have sold her soul as a child to hear. Words that would have made so many dark, scary nights so much more bearable. Words that pierced her heart like a thousand knives, because they'd come so, so late.

Tears sprang to her eyes.

And this time she let them fall.

Chapter Six

Tate gulped a quick cup of coffee. Standing in his kitchen, he stared at the big house. He'd been out where they were preparing for spring roundup all morning, making sure everything was getting set up. He'd hoped Crissy might make a foray onto the ranch over the last two days, maybe even discover roundup was about to get under way and wander out to the roundup site. But not only had he not seen her since the night of their tequila drinking, the hands working the home corrals hadn't, either. She'd obviously never left the house.

Damn. He thought she was making progress toward lightening up about her dad. About the ranch. At least she hadn't thrown his suggestion to keep the place and use it to help support her charity back in his face. A good sign.

And he'd hoped the note from her father would soften her up even more. At least he'd hoped it would make her feel less like an outsider. Make her *feel* like a beloved daughter and therefore someone who belonged here on her father's ranch.

Of course, he didn't know what Warner had written in that card. But if the man hadn't told his long lost daughter he loved her, he'd be damned surprised.

Then again, did he really expect one "I love you" to fix everything? He sighed, taking another sip of coffee. As a matter of fact, he had. He ran a hand down his face. What the hell had he been thinking? The kind of bond he'd been thinking about, the kind of bond that would make Crissy feel as if she belonged on the Big T, was not created overnight. The bond between a father and daughter grew over time. The love and trust developing as first steps were taken, first ponies ridden, first cars driven.

All Crissy had was Tate's word that her father loved her and a single card. Enough, perhaps, for a bond to begin to grow, but hardly enough to create any real sense of kinship. Any real sense of love. And if he was ever going to get her out of that house, that's what he needed to create. He needed to find a way to make her *feel* Warner's love. Not an easy task with Warner in absentia.

He took another swallow of coffee, thinking of ways to create that end. Only one came to mind. Decision made, he drained the cup with a giant gulp and headed over to the big house.

He stepped onto the porch and knocked. It seemed odd, knocking on a door he'd just walked through for the past ten years, but Warner was gone. The house was Crissy's now. She had every right to expect her privacy.

"I'll get it." Crissy's voice echoed inside.

Braxton must be there, working. He couldn't imagine who else she'd be hollering at. He heard the tread of footsteps on the stairs and a few seconds later, the door opened.

Crissy stood there, a smile curving her lips. "Hey, Tex." She was wearing a tight pair of faded jeans, hip-huggers, and a tank top that stopped just above her navel.

Heat shot through him, his gaze locked on her belly button. And the smooth expanse of skin below it. He wanted to touch her there. See if she was as soft and warm as she looked. Swallowing hard, he pulled his gaze up, made himself concentrate on her face.

She chuckled softly. "Come on in, cowboy. Looks a little warm out there."

He stepped into the house's air-conditioning, glad for whatever cooling effect he could find, and attacked the problem at hand. "Thought maybe I'd see you out on the ranch one of these days."

She shrugged, closing the door. "I've been exploring dad's office, seeing what I could learn about him."

"Then I've come just in time."

She cocked a brow in question.

"I came over to show you some things your dad left you."

"Really?" Curiosity sparkled in her eyes.

"Yep, come on." He took her elbow and guided her to the stairs, ignoring the electricity that jumped between them the second he touched her, ignoring the fact that while he was leading her upstairs for a totally innocent reason, his body seemed only to note that they were headed toward the bedrooms.

She hesitated halfway up the steps. "Where exactly are we going, Tex?" It obviously hadn't escaped her noticed that there was nothing upstairs but bedrooms.

"Relax, I'm not dragging you away to seduce you. What I want to show you is in one of your dad's closets."

"Whew, I was afraid I was going to have to pull a Jackie Chan, send you sprawling down the stairs."

He chuckled wryly. "So much for my cowboy charm, huh?"

"Oh, it's there, Tex. And we're both adult enough to know it. But now's not a good time for me to be distracted." A wry smile of her own twisted her lips. "No matter how entertaining I think that distraction might be."

More heat shot through him, his body only hearing the admission that she was as interested as he was and totally ignoring the part about this not being the time. Totally ignoring the fact that Warner's daughter was completely off-limits, period. But if his body didn't know it, his conscience did. Reluctantly, he let go of her and picked up his pace so he was a step ahead.

"So what did my father leave for me?"

"And ruin the surprise?" He shook his head. At the landing, he made his way into her father's room.

She stopped in the doorway, looking nervous and lost as she stared in. "So this was his room."

"Yep. Now quit hovering in the doorway and come in."

"I'm not hovering." Lifting her chin and squaring her shoulders, she strode in.

He hid a smile.

She wandered aimlessly for a few steps, her gaze both voracious and anxious as she drank in every detail. Spying the big eight-by-ten photograph sitting on the nightstand next to the bed, she strode over and picked it up.

Even from here he could see Warner standing in the picture with his arm around Vera's shoulders. See Vera holding a brand-new baby girl—a tiny, bald-headed Crissy—wrapped carefully in a pink blanket.

Crissy studied the photo, her expression intense. Finally, she tipped it toward him. "This was him? My father?" Her voice was whisper soft.

Surprise shot through him. "You've never seen him before?"

She shook her head. "Mom didn't have any pictures of him. Even after she died and I went through her things, there was nothing."

During all these years, she'd never had a face to put her emotions to? What the hell had Vera been thinking? Not even letting her child know what her father looked like.

Yes, from everything Warner had said, he knew the woman had had problems. And from what Crissy had told him about Vera's childhood, he could understand why she had them. But right now, he didn't care about poor Vera's problems, he just wanted to strangle her. But he managed to keep his expression neutral as he said, "That's him."

She traced the figure of her father with a shaky finger, her expression bittersweet. "He was handsome."

He chuckled. "I wouldn't know. But he was a good man. A very good man."

She didn't comment, she just continued to study the picture intently. As if she might find the answers she so needed there. "They look happy."

"I think they were when your dad wasn't busy on the ranch. But beyond what he looked like, you're not going to learn much about your dad from that picture." He strode over and took it from her, setting it back in its place. "If you want to know who your dad was, how he felt about *you,* the answers are in here."

He strode to one of the doors leading off the room, pushed it open and stepped inside the walk-in closet.

Crissy followed, once again pausing at the doorway and peering in. She took in the closet's contents in one quick sweep. "Presents?"

He nodded. "Yours. And your mother's."

She stared at the packages. "Oh, God, please tell me he didn't go out and buy all these after he found out he was dying as some sort of wish-I'd-known-you kind of thing."

"*No*. Your father was a lot of things, but a maudlin fool wasn't one of them. These are presents he bought for you and your mother over the years. Presents bought with joy and the hope that he'd find you and be able to give them to you. Yours are all birthday presents."

The shadows turned to surprise. "You're kidding. Birthday presents?"

"He always said any father worth his salt didn't miss his child's birthday."

Tears misted her eyes. "So he thought of me on my birthday. I always wondered."

Tate's heart squeezed. He couldn't imagine what it would be like to wonder if one of your parents even thought about you on your birthday. It had to be one of the loneliest feelings in the world. And loneliness, he understood. "Wonder no more. He thought of you. And not just on your birthday. All the time. Now get in here and see what he bought you."

She stepped into the closet, her gaze skating over the gifts sitting on the shelves.

The space suddenly seemed smaller, warmer, much more…intimate. He thought about bolting, leaving her to open the presents by herself. But, there were stories behind a lot of these gifts. Stories he knew. Stories she should know. So he kept his feet rooted to the floor.

Standing in front of the gifts, she touched one with a shaky finger. "This paper's old."

"It would be. It would have been wrapped the year

he got it for you. Let's see—" He reached around her—trying not to notice how close they were—and opened the little card that was taped on top and read it. "Happy seventh, sweetie."

"He wrapped this eighteen years ago?" Disbelief and something else, something tender, sounded in her voice.

"You bet." He stepped back to a safer distance.

"Amazing." She opened a few other tags, reading the inscriptions. Then she turned to one of the big presents on the floor. She angled her head, first one way and then the other, a smile playing over her lips. "Do you think this is what it looks like?"

He chuckled, looking at the way the old paper with pink teddy bears and blue balloons defined the curved bottom of the object. "I'm sure it's exactly what it looks like. You're dad told me—with great pride, I might add—how he made it himself."

"He *made* it?"

"Yep."

Her gaze softened, and she nudged the gift's highest point, sending it rocking.

He touched her shoulder. "Open it."

Uncertainty shadowed her expression as she stood, making no move toward the gift.

He hated to see her hesitancy, her doubt in her father's love. Hated more that he couldn't pull her into his arms and comfort her. But this wasn't about him. It was about her. And her relationship with Warner. "It's your present, Crissy. Your father always meant for you to open it. So open it already."

A smile crept across her lips and she gave her head a resolute nod. "All right then."

She opened the small card taped to the top. "Ride 'em, cowgirl. Happy third. Love, Dad." Her voice cracked as she read and swiped at her eyes.

Happy tears this time. Good.

She knelt beside the present and went to work on the wrapping, removing it one sheet at a time from the hodgepodge of pieces taped together to cover the big, oddly shaped object.

The process was slow and careful, as if she were unwrapping something of utmost fragility or great value. But finally, the wooden rocking horse was uncovered. "Look at it," she breathed, sitting back on her heels, staring at the handcrafted gift.

He was looking. He clamped his lips on the laugh that climbed up his throat. Warner Trevarrow had been the most talented businessman and cowboy he'd ever known. But he'd been a sad excuse for a woodworker.

He stared at the poor wooden horse. The rockers were good; Warner must have used a pattern for those. But the rest of the horse… He stifled another laugh. Any horse whose legs were that crooked had best be a rocking horse, 'cause he sure as blazes wasn't walking anywhere. Which, considering the position of the animal's eyes, one almost two inches lower than the other, was probably just as well. The poor beast had to be seeing double. And there was a giant gouge in one haunch, as if Warner's carving tool had slipped. He swallowed another laugh. The poor, poor beast.

"It's beautiful." The words were filled with quiet reverence as Crissy reached out to touch the polished surface.

This time, he couldn't stop the laugh. It bubbled out like water from a spring. "Are you blind?"

She reached behind her and slapped at his leg. "Stop it. He *is* beautiful."

He laughed harder. "For crying out loud, the animal looks like something Rudolph the red-nosed reindeer would have found on the island of misfits. And undoubtedly left there."

She smiled with him now. "Maybe, but that's what makes him beautiful. If he was perfect, how would I know for sure my dad made him? But look—" she ran her hand over the dimple in the horse's butt "—there's no mistaking it."

No there wasn't.

She ran her fingers over the tooled leather pad that had been fixed to the horse's back with brass upholstery tacks. "Look at this. He must have spent hours." Awe sounded in her voice.

Tate marveled at the depth of tenderness with which she touched the horse. Considering the hardships she'd endured because of her father's mistake, considering she'd spent years thinking of the man as the bad guy, she could easily have looked at the poorly crafted horse and wondered why her father hadn't spent a little cash and bought his daughter a rocking horse without a dimple in its butt.

But it wasn't the gift itself she was appreciating. It

was the time her father had spent making it for her. The effort he had put into it that meant something to her. That distinction told him a great deal about the woman kneeling in front of him. Told him that she knew what was important in life and what wasn't. Told him that she had a big capacity for forgiveness, because all he had to do was look at the expression on her face to know she'd let go of the anger she'd had for her father. Not such an easy thing when one considered the hardships she'd lived through. Many of them that could be laid directly at Warner's feet.

She was a hell of a woman. Beautiful. Tough. Forgiving.

Desire shot through him, hot and hard and greedy. Desire that went much deeper than the biting lust he'd felt before.

He closed his eyes against it. He might once have dreamed of having a woman like Crissy at his side. Dreamed of building a family with a strong, loving woman. But those days, those dreams were behind him. He'd thrown them away the day he'd taken the law into his own hands. And he couldn't get them back.

Ruthlessly ignoring the need pounding through him, he forced his thoughts back to the moment. "Actually, according to your father, he spent weeks putting this guy together."

"Weeks." She glanced over her shoulder, a telltale sheen of moisture in her eyes. "You could have shown me all these gifts the first day I came."

He shook his head. "I wanted you to be able to appreciate them. Enjoy them. And I was pretty sure that's not how you would have looked at them that first day."

"No. I wouldn't have." She touched the end of the horse's nose, then looked back at him. "Thanks."

"No problem." He held his hand down to her. "Come on, let's open some more."

"Yeah, let's." Smiling from ear to ear, she grabbed his hand and pulled herself up. She surveyed the shelves, homing in on a rectangular box about eighteen inches high. After a quick check of the tag she pulled it off the shelf. "Let's try this one. He bought this the year I was ten."

He smiled. She looked about ten now, her eyes glistening with anticipation as she ripped the paper from the box.

She pulled the last of the paper away. "Yeah, baby." She turned the box so he could see. "Barbie."

He stared at the big-busted, tiny-waisted figure. "Yep, that looks like her." He'd never understood the love affair the entire female population under the age of twelve seemed to have with the doll, but he'd known enough little girls in his life to know it was real.

She turned the box around and ran her finger over the clear plastic, studying the doll. "I can't believe it. A new Barbie. Look, her hair is perfect. And so is her dress. Not a single tear or stain."

"I take it there weren't a lot of new Barbies in your childhood."

She shook her head. "Toys and clothes always came

from garage sales or Goodwill. Which, on the whole, is fine. You can get some pretty neat stuff at garage sales. But I gotta tell you, finding a Barbie in halfway decent shape was tough. The hair and clothes were always a mess. But this one…" She ran her fingers over the plastic again, her gaze almost beatific as she stared at the doll.

"So open her up. Take her out."

Her fingers moved to the top of the box, but at the last second they stilled and she shook her head. "I think I'll keep her just the way she is—all shiny and new in her pink box. Maybe I'll give her to my little girl. That would be cool, a Barbie bought by her grand-dad."

Her little girl. He pictured her holding a tiny baby with blond hair and green eyes. Pictured himself making that baby with her, a fresh wave of need pounding through him. He gritted his teeth against it. And fisted his hands against the thought of someone *else* making that baby with her. Fisted them harder as he realized sooner or later someone else would. Because while Crissy deserved a fairy-tale ending, complete with Prince Charming and a couple of kids, he didn't belong anywhere in that picture. No one would mistake him for Prince Charming.

He forced the images of making love to Crissy out of his head and concentrated on the moment at hand.

Crissy set the Barbie carefully back on the shelf and did a quick read of a few tags before picking up the next present and turning to him. "Shall we see what's in this one? It says Sweet Sixteen, Sweetie."

Though short, the messages on the tiny cards obviously meant as much to her as the gifts. "Open away."

She tore the wrapping away, revealing a square, thin, white velvet box.

He smiled. "Looks like jewelry to me."

Her eyes sparkling, she opened the box. "Oh, my God." She tipped the box so he could see.

A single strand of white pearls glistened in the closet's light.

"Very pretty. But they'll be prettier on."

"You think?" Hesitancy sounded in her voice, as if she couldn't quite believe they were hers.

He nodded. "Definitely."

She lifted the pearls from their velvet bed with unsteady fingers. Setting the box down, she opened the clasp on the pearls and fit it around her neck. But her fingers weren't steady enough to connect the clasp.

He shouldn't help. The last thing he needed was to be close enough to touch her. But before he knew it, his feet were moving across the closet floor, and he was saying, "Here, let me get that."

Stupid. Stupid, stupid, *stupid*. But his hands were already taking the tiny gold clasp from hers. His fingers drinking in her warmth, reveling in the soft silkiness of her nape.

He steeled himself against the desire racing through him. Told himself he was only offering a helping hand. But the tightening of his jeans belied that reasoning. He wanted to touch her. Wanted to feel her.

Foolish.

And dangerous.

He promised himself he'd step away as soon as he had the necklace hooked. But he had the clasp locked in seconds. And his feet didn't move. Nor did his hands move from her neck.

Instead, they settled on her shoulders, molding to her soft curves, his fingers stretching to the delicate line of her collarbone. And his feet took another half step closer, his body touching hers, measuring her curves, reveling in her softness.

She stilled, the air around them becoming super-charged, crackling with electricity and latent desire.

He prayed for her to move away. Because, damn his soul, he couldn't. He couldn't make his feet move. Couldn't make his hands let go any more than a dying man could make himself forgo that last sip of sweet air.

With his own bleak future stretching before him, he wanted to taste her generous spirit. Wanted to taste her incredible strength. He didn't want to think of the cold, lonely years ahead of him. Didn't want to think about how solitary his current existence was.

She didn't move away. And when she looked over her shoulder at him, she didn't look the least bit in-clined to move. Her eyes were slightly dilated. Her lips parted. Her breathing short and fast. God help him, she looked like a woman ready to be kissed.

A loud ringing chime peeled through the house.

They both started, the sound breaking the spell.

She sprang out of his hands as if she'd been burned,

her cheeks coloring a becoming shade of pink. "That's the, um…"

He dropped his hands and stepped back with a wry smile. "The doorbell. Go on, answer it. I'll be right behind you."

She dashed out of the closet.

He followed at a more sedate pace, giving his body time to cool, telling himself the interruption was for the best. He had no business touching Crissy Albreit. No matter how much he wanted to.

He found her at the door, holding a simple green vase with a dozen red roses in it and talking to the flower deliveryman—or boy. The pimply-faced kid couldn't be more than eighteen.

She handed the teenager a five-dollar tip, said thanks, and closed the door as he disappeared down the stairs. Turning to Tate, she held the flowers up. "Will you look at these?" She stuck her nose into the blooms and took a deep breath, her eyes closing as she inhaled the scent. "Beautiful. But who on earth is sending me roses?"

He knew, and wished he hadn't been here for their arrival.

But before he could leave, she pulled the card from the clear plastic holder and opened it. "Just a little nudge to get you thinking about planting those red roses." She looked up, shaking her head. "Not fair, cowboy."

As if he needed any reminders at the moment of how unfair life could be. Ruthlessly ignoring the need still throbbing inside him, he stopped at the door and locked his gaze on hers. "Life doesn't give second chances often, Crissy. But you're being offered one now. A chance to get to know your dad. A chance to make a good future for yourself. Don't throw it away." Without another word he brushed by her and headed back to his house.

His quiet, empty house.

Chapter Seven

Early the next morning Crissy stood next to the table where she'd set McCade's roses, her nose buried in the burgundy blooms. They smelled so good. Bold, sweet…heady.

Much like the man who'd sent them.

Smiling ruefully, she took another deep whiff and straightened, trying not to let her mind wander, once again, back to the thoughts that had kept her awake most of the night. Thoughts of Tate McCade.

But it was impossible.

She couldn't get the man out of her head. Couldn't get the heat of him standing behind her, his hard body brushing hers, out of her mind. He'd almost kissed her last night.

And she'd almost let him.

Not good.

She needed a clear head for the decision ahead of her—whether she was going to make the Big T her home. And she needed that decision to be unbiased and well-grounded. She couldn't let herself decide to stay on the ranch just because McCade made her heart pound and her palms sweat. Even if he did seem to have a depth to him, a tenderness she'd never seen in a man before.

If she was going to stay on the Big T, make it her home, it had to be because it was right for her. With the issues about her father cleared up, it certainly had potential. But if she decided to stay, it had to be because of the ranch—not the man.

Of course, if she decided the Big T was the place for her in a totally unbiased and well-grounded manner, McCade would be fair game. Right?

Lord, she was hopeless. She walked over to the big window behind the table and stared out at the open vista behind the house.

The day was just starting, the pink rays of dawn glinting off the hills. God, it was beautiful here. The thought of staying, making it her home, planting those roses pulled sweetly at her. The thought of finally, *finally,* having a real home was an intoxicating elixir. One she'd have to be careful of.

Because the reality was she didn't know anything about this ranch, except she liked the scenery and her father had once owned it. She'd have to know a lot more than that before she made any real decision about staying. *And as long as you're standing around twiddling your thumbs, girl, you're not going to know anything. Get outta here and go see what this place has to offer.* She pivoted away from the window and headed for the kitchen. After the sleepless night she'd had, she was in dire need of a little caffeine.

Five minutes later, full mug in hand, she headed onto the porch. The early morning Texas air sent goose bumps dancing over her skin. Pulling the door shut behind her, she took a sip of coffee and peered out over the ranch. It had been quieter the last few days at the corrals here by the house.

Across the way, the door to McCade's house opened and he strode out.

"Hey, Tex." Without the usual hustle and bustle, she barely had to raise her voice for the words to carry across the road.

He swung his gaze to the big house, spotting her immediately. He froze midstride, the corners of his mouth tipping down and his brows scrunching together.

She wondered if he was thinking of yesterday's almost-kiss, too. Wondered if he regretted the interruption or was glad for it.

But before she could discern any real idea of his thoughts from his expression, he smoothed his face into an inscrutable mask. "You're up early."

"Actually, I never went to sleep." So he was going to pretend the almost-kiss hadn't happened.

Okay with her. While she didn't understand why he

was as reserved about the attraction growing between them as she was, his reservation certainly made life easier. The man was hard enough to resist as it was. If he was actually trying to pursue her…she'd be sunk. So she'd let him get away with pretending nothing had happened yesterday. For now, anyway.

He strode across the dirt road and joined her on her father's porch. "Another sleepless night?"

She held up her mug. "Thank God for caffeine."

He chuckled, raising his thermos. "Amen to that."

She tried desperately not to notice the spicy scent of his aftershave, the sensuous line of his lips. "A thermos, huh? That looks like a man going to work. Where are you heading?"

"To one of the outer pastures. It's spring roundup. The cowboys have been gathering the cows for the last week and today we start working them. Wanna come? Be a great way for you to see what the Big T is all about."

"So that's where everyone is."

He nodded. "Gonna join us?"

Did she want to? She'd decided to look things over, but she'd been thinking more along the lines of checking things out from afar, staying below the radar of the ranch's workers. If she headed out to the roundup, she'd be in the middle of a lot of men who were no doubt wondering how she was going to affect their future. Men who had definite opinions about her father— and undoubtedly her mother as well. It could be pretty uncomfortable.

Then again, as McCade had pointed out, it would be a great way to see what the Big T was about. "So what happens at spring roundup? Is this when you ship the cows off to market?"

He shook his head. "That's fall roundup, after the herds have fattened up on summer pastures. Right now, we're vaccinating, branding, castrating and doing a general health check."

She thought of the westerns she'd seen on television. Roundup had always been depicted as an exciting event. Seeing one in person sounded like fun. "Yeah, I wanna go."

He tipped his head toward his truck. "Let's do it then." He strode off the porch.

She followed, hurrying to keep up with his longer stride. "You're not riding out?"

"We keep the horses out with the herds during roundup and drive back and forth from the site. That way, the horses can save their energy for working the cattle."

She crawled into the truck, careful not to spill her coffee. "That makes sense, but riding would have been more fun."

He smiled, putting the truck in gear. "We can saddle a horse for you once we get out there if you like."

"If there's time, that might be nice."

Once they were headed down the road, he cast another glance her way. "So does this little foray mean you've decided to give the place a chance?"

"Well, let's say I'm thinking about it."

He chuckled softly. "Careful, you wouldn't want to commit yourself."

She took a sip of coffee, smiling. "It's not as easy as you want it to be, Tex. While you've calmed the loyalty issues I had about the place, convinced me my father loved me and that what happened twenty-two years ago was a big, ugly mistake both my parents were responsible for, I still don't want to jump into something that isn't right for me."

"And no one would want you to. But, I have to admit, you seem a little more cautious than I would anticipate for someone who spends her free time jumping out of helicopters with no parachute."

"That's different. The Angel stunts are a small part of my life. The Big T wouldn't be small. And after finding myself in a bad situation three years ago, I—"

He looked over, his brows pulled low in worry.

She waved away his concern. "Nothing life threatening or serious. Just…icky stuff. You know, a rundown apartment, a job I hated and a boyfriend who was playing around on me."

"Sounds pretty dismal."

"It was. And the worst thing about it was that I was suffering through the first two things for the last thing."

"The apartment and job for the snaky boyfriend?"

"Yeah." She shook her head. "What was I thinking? I *know* better. Until my mom got too sick to play the field, I watched her go from one man who really didn't care for her to the next. Men who were just using her for free rent, free sex, free whatever they needed at the time that she was happy to give to them in exchange for a little affection. It made me crazy. And I promised myself, time and time again, I wouldn't fall into that pattern."

"But you did."

"Oh yeah. Lock, stock and barrel. But when I found out Tom was playing around on me while I paid the rent, I realized what I was doing. And I drew the line. I promised myself I wasn't going to waste one more day waiting for someone else to make me happy. I was going to make myself happy. I was going to find out what I wanted to do in life—and do it."

"And how's that going?"

She laughed. "Well, part of it's going really well. I love the Angels stuff. The girls are like the sisters I never had. And when I'm snowboarding or learning a new stunt for a fund-raiser, life sparkles. The boredom, the…I don't know, the lack of direction in my everyday life disappears. And doing something for someone who needs it, someone like Chad…it's the best feeling in the world. Even the excitement of the stunts pales in comparison.

"But, like I said, that's a small part of my life. And the rest of it… Let's just say being a waitress at the local pie house, which is how I'm currently support-ing myself, is *not* something I want to do forever. I'm going to college, taking classes in business, but I can't really picture myself in the business world, either."

"Then why are you taking business classes? Why not take something else?"

She chuckled. "Because I have yet to find any classes that capture my interest. And because I thought I could at least use some of what I was learning in business classes with the charity. We've just recently started to sell a few Alpine Angels items, T-shirts, coffee mugs, that kind of thing. We're hoping to develop a more constant supply of money for the charity. And I figured knowing more about business couldn't hurt. But the thought of spending my day sitting at a desk…" She shivered just thinking about it.

"Well, if college isn't giving you the direction you want, maybe the Big T will."

"Maybe it will. I'd be lying if I said the prospect of staying here wasn't a little thrilling. I like the idea of the steady flow of money for the charity. And I love animals. Dogs, cats, horses, cows, mice—I've never met a furry friend I didn't like. *But,* I suspect having a few pets is a far cry from running a ranch that raises animals for profit. And I'm not going to jump into something just because it's handy. Or because I think my father would have wanted me to. If I stay, it has to be because *I* want it."

"And no one, least of all your father, would want it any other way."

While she didn't take that to mean McCade wouldn't do everything in his power to make her love the place, she did take it to mean he wouldn't hog-tie her and throw her into a closet just to keep her here. Which had to be a major concession on his part. She gave him a single nod. "Okay, then."

He returned her nod with a succinct one of his own. "Okay, then."

As the truck moved over the dirt roads that seemed to wind throughout the ranch, she sipped at her coffee and stole an occasional glance at McCade. She couldn't stop staring at those lips. Couldn't stop wondering what they would have felt like on hers if only the delivery boy hadn't shown up. Couldn't stop wondering about the man himself.

She forced herself to turn her head and look out the side window. She was *not* going to think about that kiss. She was *not* going to wonder if McCade had been born around here, if he had a family nearby, or a girlfriend. Those things were none of her business.

Except…

He *was* the foreman of this ranch. If she stayed, shouldn't she know something about the men who worked for her?

Of course she should.

In fact, it was her *responsibility* to know the men. She turned back to McCade. "So, tell me about yourself, Tex. Tell me about your family, your mom and dad. Do they live nearby?"

He stilled, tension filling his frame.

Odd. He was so dedicated to her father she would have thought he'd be close to his own family. But if the current silence meant anything, such wasn't the case.

Finally, he said, "They live a couple towns over." There was a tightness in his voice that clearly indicated there wasn't anything casual about the subject for him.

She briefly debated changing the subject, but he certainly hadn't been shy about pushing her to look at unpleasant events in her past. "How close is a couple towns over? Do you get to see them much?"

A muscle in his jaw ticked. A beat of silence. Then… "The Big T keeps me pretty busy, not much time for visiting."

"I see. What about brothers and sisters? Have any?"

He looked away, but not quickly enough to hide his frown. "No."

She cocked her head, studying him. What could possibly be so upsetting about being an only child?

She was formulating just the right question when McCade pointed out the window, relief in his voice. "Here we are."

She shifted her gaze out the windshield. Lucky for him, they had indeed arrived. A medium-sized valley opened up before them. A valley filled with cows and horses and men. Her questions for McCade momentarily diverted, she stared wide-eyed at the chaos before her.

There were several wooden corrals set up in the area. Some big, some small. Some filled with cows. Some empty. Campfires burned here and there, smoke curling gently from the small, well-contained flames. Two of them, one at each end of the valley, had metal grates and coffeepots poised over them. The other fires had long metal rods with wooden handles sticking out. Branding irons, she imagined.

Cowboys were everywhere, herding cows, chasing

strays, setting up corrals and congregating in small bands here and there, no doubt deciding what to do next.

And the noise. Hundreds of cows mooing, hooves pounding the hard-packed earth and cowboys whistling and shouting at each other and the cows as they went about their business.

Wow. A shiver of excitement slid through her. Maybe she had found a home.

Her attention caught on four cowboys pulling a big metal gate out of a pickup. Their muscles rippled as they lifted the heavy piece off the truck's battered bed. She smiled. There was a definite item for the pro side of staying. Cowboys 24/7. None of them as handsome as McCade, but pretty great scenery nonetheless.

Pulling her gaze from the cowboys, she looked to McCade. Definitely the cutest of the lot. "Okay, this is pretty damned impressive."

"It's an impressive ranch, thanks to your dad. Come on."

She followed him out, the sounds no longer muffled by the truck, exploding around her. The smell of dust and livestock flooded her senses.

The ground shook beneath her feet. *Shook.*

She looked over at McCade, amazement pouring through her. She pointed to her feet and pitched her voice over the cacophony of sound. "I can feel the cows thundering around."

He smiled. "You bet. Come on, I'll introduce you

to some of the men." He strode toward a campfire, one of the fires with coffeepots over the flames.

Trepidation ran through her at the prospect of meeting the men, but the excitement of the moment helped keep it at bay as she followed him.

He stepped up to the group, waving a hand toward her. "Gentlemen, this is Crissy Albreit. Crissy, Tommy Ray Bartel, Corey Richardson and you know Braxton."

Every hat came off as they shifted their gazes to her.

Apparently, chivalry wasn't dead in the cowboy culture. She smiled, nodding a good morning to Braxton. "No books this morning, huh?"

He shook his head. "Every once in a while, a little fresh air is required."

"You'll get no argument from me there." She turned to the nearest cowboy and held out her hand. "Mr. Bartel."

The tall, blond cowboy smiled, his shaggy hair rustling in the morning breeze as he closed his big, callused hand over hers. "Mr. Bartel is my daddy, ma'am. I'm just Tommy Ray." His thick, sweet accent said Texas son through and through. And the set of dimples that smile set off… Almost as arresting as those big, blue, Bambi-shaped eyes.

Man, where did a man get eyes like that? She preferred the intensity of McCade's brown ones, but she imagined any number of women swooned at this cowboy's feet. "Tommy Ray it is." Releasing his hand she turned to the other man—make that teenager, around sixteen she'd guess—and held her hand out. "Corey."

While Tommy Ray's expression had been open and easy, Corey's eyes held much of the unease she'd seen in the faces of the men around the corrals. But he took her hand and bobbed his head politely. "Ma'am, pleased to meet you."

As if he sensed both her and the boy's unease, McCade turned to Braxton, moving the conversation along. "You bring Blackie out with you this morning?"

"You bet."

"How's he doing?"

Braxton lifted his coffee cup toward one of the corrals holding horses. "Good. For a youngster at his first roundup, damn good. He's working the cows great."

"Well, let's see. I brought Crissy out to impress her. Convince her what a great place this would be to live. So let's show her what a good cutting pony can do."

Braxton smiled ruefully, tossing the coffee left in his cup on the fire. "That's what I like, no pressure." He looked to Crissy. "Ever seen a cutting horse in action?"

"Nope. But I'm looking forward to it."

"Well, let's hope we don't disappoint. Come on, gentlemen."

Tommy Ray and Corey downed their coffee in big swallows and the three cowboys headed off.

For the first time she took a good look at the cows around her. Their dark red coats gleamed richly in the sun. "God, they're beautiful. And enormous. In Colorado, we have a lot of Herefords, but they aren't nearly as massive as these guys."

"No, they aren't. But then the Santa Gertrudis is one of the largest cattle breeds around."

"They must be, even the babies are big and stocky. Look at the wrinkles under that one's neck." She pointed to a baby standing by his mom. "Too cute."

He chuckled. "Your dad liked all those wrinkles, too. In fact, he loved everything about this breed. Which is no doubt why he raised some of the best Santa Gertrudis breeding stock in the country."

Just then, Braxton and Tommy Ray rode into view, carrying coiled ropes in their free hands.

"Where's Corey?" she asked.

McCade pointed to one of the fires with the branding irons. "He'll be the one administering vaccines and doing the branding. It'll be Tommy Ray's and Braxton's jobs to catch the calves and get them ready for him."

She shifted her gaze back to Tommy Ray and Braxton.

"Here they go," Tate said.

Braxton and Tommy Ray had reached the herd. They rode along the edge of the bovine gathering as if looking for just the right cow. Suddenly Blackie was a blur of motion. He leaped forward, his front feet hitting the ground together. Dropping his shoulders, he stretched his neck out and pinned his ears against his head.

Cows and horse dodged first one way and then another. She didn't have any idea which cow the horse was trying to cut out, but Blackie seemed to know. He bounced like a lightning bolt from one spot to the next, Braxton sitting perfectly still in the saddle.

It looked like fun. Way fun. She'd love to give that a try.

As suddenly as the action had begun a mama cow and her baby broke away from the herd.

Tommy Ray, who'd been standing quietly by while Braxton and Blackie separated the mama and baby from the others, went into action. He booted his horse into a gallop and ran beside the calf and mama, keeping the animals from veering away from Braxton. Blackie staying hot on the cows' heels, Braxton swung a lasso over his head, flipped his wrist and sent the giant circle sailing. It flew through the air and settled over the calf's head.

Braxton pulled Blackie to a skidding halt, securing his end of the rope to the saddle's horn. The calf quickly hit the end of the rope's play, snapping back. Before the horse had even quit sliding in the dusty Texas dirt, Braxton vaulted from the saddle and jogged toward the calf.

McCade tipped his head toward the action. "Watch the way the horse backs up, keeping the rope tight so the calf can't get away."

Sure enough, even without the rider's guidance, Blackie backed up a step or two keeping any slack from forming between the horse and calf as Braxton ran to the calf, flipped him over and tied three of his legs together with a smaller rope he pulled out of his back pocket.

Adrenaline shot through her. If the last thirty seconds meant anything, living here could be an exciting way to spend her life.

The bound calf bawled loudly. The mother bawled louder, as if to protest the treatment of her baby. Or perhaps to let him know he wasn't alone.

The plaintive calls pulled at her heart. "Poor baby."

"He's okay. And it's all for his own good." He waved a hand toward Corey, who was running toward Braxton with something in his hand. "First, the vaccines."

As Braxton held the calf steady, Corey uncapped syringes and quickly injected the calf with the vaccines that would keep him healthy. Then he jogged back to the fire, tossed the used syringes into a bucket and pulled one of the rods out of the fire.

She winced at the cherry-red T glowing on the end of the branding iron. "Ooh, I'm not going to like this."

"Don't look then. It's quick. He'll be back with his mom in no time."

She closed her eyes, but, like someone driving by an accident, couldn't resist a peek. She cracked her eyelids just as the brand connected with the calf's flank.

Flames leaped from the end of the brand where the T met the calf's hide. The calf's frightened bawl turned to a scream of pain, his small, brown eyes going wide and rolling in their sockets.

She took a step back, her stomach turning. The acrid smell of burned fur and flesh filled her senses. Oh, God.

Now she closed her eyes. Tight. But the sound of the bawling calf kept the picture firmly implanted in her head.

Strong hands closed over her shoulders. "Easy. It's over. He's fine. Look, he's running to his mom for a drink."

She opened her eyes just enough to peek through. The calf was indeed racing to his mom. As soon as he reached her, he stuck his head under her and grabbed a teat. A small sigh of relief whispered through her and she opened her eyes all the way. "That's awful. Isn't there a better way to mark these guys?"

"Branding is the quickest. And the most cost-efficient."

She shivered. "It's barbaric."

Another calf screamed behind her.

She whipped around to find the process going on at one of the other campfires. A small calf had been hog-tied and a cowboy was holding him down as the brand burned into his flesh. Every sensibility in her exploded. "Stop it." The hollered words carried over the melee.

The cowboys looked up from their chore.

"Stop it," she hollered again.

Surprise flashed across their faces as the brand lifted from the calf's flank, but the cowboys didn't let the young animal go.

"Let him up," she hollered, her hands balled into fists at her sides. *"Let him up."*

Clearly astounded by her outburst, they looked to McCade.

"Don't look at him. He's not the boss here. I am. *Let the calf go.*" She started toward them. She'd pull the calf out of their hold if she had to.

McCade strode after her, grabbing her arm and pulling her back. "Crissy, wait."

She jerked away. "*No.* I'm not waiting. On the plane, you were the one who said I was the boss here. Am I or not?"

His lips pressed into a thin line, but he nodded toward the men.

They released the calf, and the little fellow went running to his mom, but the cowboys' gazes never left her.

She nodded toward the rod still in the cowboy's hand. "Put the damned branding iron down and kick dirt over that fire. And every other one in the valley that doesn't have a coffeepot over it. There's not going to be any more branding here, got it?"

The cowboys looked at her like she was crazy. And the valley seemed suddenly quiet.

She looked around. The cows were still mooing, but the cowboys were no longer hollering back and forth. They were all standing or sitting quietly on their horses, staring at her.

Next to her McCade swore softly. "Crissy—"

"Don't Crissy me." She snapped her gaze to his. "Tell them to put out the damned fires and pack up and go home."

"Stupid." The whispered comment came from behind her.

She swung around to find Corey glaring at her from beneath his cowboy hat. She narrowed her eyes on him. "Excuse me?"

Anger darkened the boy's gaze. "I said—"

"Corey, that's enough," McCade hissed.

"No, it's not enough," the teenager spat. "What does she know about cattle? She comes here, and she's going to ruin everything for everyone. Why doesn't she just go back where she came from? She doesn't belong here."

The boy's words hit her like a punch to the gut. He was right. No matter how much her father might have wanted it, she hadn't been raised on this ranch. She didn't know anything about cows or ranching.

McCade put his hand on her shoulder. "Crissy—"

She pushed his hand off. "Forget it." She'd hoped briefly that this could be her home. But torturing little animals wasn't what she wanted to do with her life. She'd been right about owning a few pets and running a ranch for profit being different. And she was definitely not cut out for the latter. "The boy's right, Tex. I don't belong here."

"Yes, you do."

She looked at the men scattered around the valley. They were still staring at her, shock or anger or disdain filling their expressions. McCade might want her to stay because he'd promised her father he'd bring her home, but every other man in this valley knew she didn't belong here.

She turned back to McCade. "No, I don't. But until I leave, everyone's going to have to put up with me.

Send these cows back to the range. The next owner can worry about torturing the poor beasts."

He swore under his breath, his look intense as he closed the distance between them. "Put the branding on hold if you want, but we need to vaccinate or we'll have sick, dying animals." His voice was as intense as his look, but he kept it low, so only she would hear.

"Fine. Vaccinate and do whatever medical procedures you need to keep the animals healthy. But that's it." She spun on her heel, strode to McCade's truck and crawled in the driver's seat. Thank God he'd left the keys in the ignition. Two seconds later, she was headed out of torment valley.

Chapter Eight

"Can you give me directions to the site?" Crissy wrote the roads and highways the man on the other end of the line gave her on the margin in the phone book, said thanks and hung up.

She was getting off this ranch. At least for a little while. She'd spent what was left of yesterday after she'd driven in from the roundup and all of today hiding in her room, doing her best to avoid Braxton and any other cowboy who might wander into the house on business.

She hadn't wanted to face any of them, hadn't wanted to see anyone else looking at her the way the cowboys on the range had yesterday morning. As if she were some lunatic come to ruin their lives. But she couldn't take one more minute of confinement.

McCade, of course, had tried to talk her out of her room once, but she'd refused to listen to him, turning the radio up so she couldn't hear him talking through the door. Listening to him would have been too dangerous. Not just because she thought staying wasn't in her best interest, but because she was afraid she'd consider staying…just to be around McCade. Definitely not good.

So she'd stayed barricaded in her room. But she couldn't take it anymore. She needed to get out. Blow some steam. And that was exactly what she was going to do.

She slipped on her tennies, grabbed a sweater, tore the page with the directions scribbled on it out of the phone book and zipped out of her room. At ten o'clock at night, she shouldn't have any problem avoiding everyone.

Tate put the phone down. He finally had the ammunition he needed to pry Crissy out of that damned room. At least he hoped he did. He sure wasn't going to convince her what happened on the range the other morning was no big deal if she kept herself locked up. He stepped out onto his porch, the night surrounding him.

The sound of a truck's engine broke the night's silence.

He looked over to the big house in time to see the headlights of Warner's truck flick on. Huh-oh. Looked like Crissy was sneaking away. Not good. "Crissy!"

She either didn't hear his holler or she was ignoring him, because the truck started to pull away.

He dashed across the road, quickly stepping in front of the vehicle before it got up any real speed.

With the tall yard light shining through her windshield, he could see her eyes go wide. Then the truck skidded to a halt just inches from him.

He breathed a little sigh of relief. Considering her mood last time he'd seen her, he hadn't been certain she wouldn't just gun it and run him down. Considering the look on her face right now, she still might.

She jammed the truck into Park and banged the steering wheel with her fists. Then she stabbed the window button, sending the window whirring down. "What the *heck* do you think you're doing, jumping in front of me like that?"

"Trying to stop you from making a quick getaway. Going any place in particular?" He spread his feet and hung his hands on his hips, making as much of a barricade as he could with his body.

She looked heavenward. "Like it's any of your business."

He didn't budge. "Where are you going, Crissy?"

"Oh, for pity's sake, I'm not heading to the airport if that's what you're worried about. The will says I have to stay six months. I'll be here six months."

"Then what's the harm in telling me where you're going?"

She narrowed her eyes and glared at him through the windshield.

He stared back.

He could see the moment she realized he wasn't budging until she coughed up her destination. She hissed in exasperation. "I'm heading to Dawson's Gorge. Any problem with that?"

"Dawson's Gorge? At ten o'clock at night?" Dawson's Gorge was two towns over, and, to his knowledge, the town's biggest attraction was the gas station on the corner. It closed at six. "What are you going there for?"

"Apparently that gorge is big enough to offer a little fun. They've got moonlight bungee jumping for those who are interested. And I'm interested. Now get out of my way."

"*Moonlight—* Oh, for crying out loud." He shouldn't be surprised at her destructive behavior. But he was certainly disappointed by it. He stomped around to the driver's window. "You have a bad day and you rush off to see if you can get yourself killed?"

"Oh, please, you're blowing things way out of proportion, cowboy. Bungee jumping is one of the safest sports around. If I wanted to kill myself I'd…I'd—"

"Jump out of a helicopter from fifty feet up and try to ski down a mountain that carries not one single human footprint?" Sarcasm dripped from his words.

"Oh, come on, I've been skiing and snowboarding for years. And doing it in the backcountry, since ski slopes cost money and mountains are free."

"Don't try to compare whatever backcountry skiing you did as a kid to the mountains I saw you girls scream down in Alaska. They're nowhere near the same and you know it. One little mistake from any point on that run and you could have broken every bone in your body."

A hint of a smile tugged at her lips. "Well, I might have done that. But you have to remember that's why they donate the big bucks."

Anger slashed through him. "This isn't funny, dammit."

She rocked back, surprised at his vehemence. But hot on the heel of surprise came another reaction. Her expression softened. "Were you worried about me that day?"

"Hell, yes, I was worried. You think I like watching four girls try to kill themselves?"

"We weren't trying to kill ourselves, Tex. We were trying to save a little boy." Her tone was easy now, gently coaxing.

He wasn't swayed. "Yes, you were. But there are a million other themes you could have used for that fundraiser. A million *safe* themes. But you chose a death-defying stunt instead. If you think that doesn't point to a death wish, you need to step back and take a better look."

She cocked her head, studying him, her gaze intense. "Why do I get the distinct impression you aren't spouting some psychological theory you've picked up from a book somewhere? Did someone you know... have a death wish?"

A cold sweat coated his skin. Old memories rushed

in. He ruthlessly closed them out. "It doesn't take a psychologist to know that anyone who flirts with the kind of danger the Alpine Angels rush into on a regular basis are fighting...*something*. Or running from it."

She sighed. "The only thing I'm running from right now is you. And a bunch of other cowboys who would undoubtedly just as soon see the back of me."

"Now *you're* blowing things out of proportion. Quit turning what happened on the range yesterday into some big event."

"It *was* a big event, Tex. I hated what I saw there. *And* I made a complete idiot of myself in front of every cowboy out there. It was a disaster."

"A disaster?" He laughed humorlessly. "A disaster is a stampede that leaves dead calves and cowboys in its wake. Or a freak storm that drops temperatures and a foot of snow in the middle of calving. Or a disease that sweeps through the herd, taking life and profits with it. *Those* are disasters."

"Well, with any luck I won't be around long enough to experience any of those delightful scenarios."

Trying to reason with her obviously wasn't going to get the job done. Time for a different approach. "So you're giving up on the place, just like that?"

"Not just like that. I gave it a chance. I *wanted* it to work. It just didn't. Realistically, we both knew it probably wouldn't."

"*I* knew no such thing. I still don't know it. And after ten minutes on the range, I don't know how you can possibly know it, either." He shook his head. "I can't believe Warner's daughter is this much of a quitter."

His metaphorical kick in the butt hit dead center. Outrage slashed across her face. "I'm not a quitter. I told you I wasn't going to settle for a job I didn't like. And trust me when I tell you I didn't like what I saw yesterday at roundup. *And* since you're pointing out my faults, I'd like to point out that name-calling isn't the most mature behavior I've ever seen."

"Neither is running away at the first sign of trouble. And that's what you're doing here."

She grimaced. "I told you the other day how important it was for me to find a job that would make me happy."

"And I applaud you for that. But if you think you're going to find a job where you love everything about it, you're dreaming. Everything in life has a downside. Unfortunately, yesterday you saw the downside. Tonight, I want to show you the upside."

"What? You found some more animals you want to torture in front of me? A few cowboys who don't think I'm a lunatic yet?"

"Come on, Crissy, can the histrionics and give the place one more chance."

"Give me one good reason why I should."

He tipped his hat back and locked his gaze on hers. "Because yesterday morning you wanted the Big T to work out for you. Because you *want* a home."

"Yeah, well, I'd like to wake up tomorrow morning

to world peace and universal health care, but I don't think it's going to happen."

"Maybe not. But if you thought there was even a chance you could bring either of those things about, would you give up on them?"

"No, I wouldn't." She gave a long, resigned sigh. "You're a devious man, Tate McCade."

"Just determined. Come on, you'll like this. I promise." He opened her door and waited patiently beside it.

With more defeat than enthusiasm, she turned the ignition off. "Fine. Where are we going?"

He gave her a hand down from the truck's cab, the sexual tension starting its inevitable upward climb the moment their fingers touched. He let go of her the second her feet hit the ground. "The barn. One of our mares is about to foal."

"A baby horse? Really?" Excitement bubbled through her.

"Yep, Hank just called, said the time has arrived." He shut the door behind her and struck out across the yard, his fingers still tingling from her touch. Great.

He'd known it wouldn't be easy, even with the foal's help, to convince her to stay. Now he realized the real trick might be in convincing her to stay without letting things get out of control the way they had the other day in the closet.

He shoved his hands in his pockets, determined to get a hold of his libido. And his emotions. Almost kissing her the other day had been a mistake. A big mistake. One he couldn't let happen again.

Crissy lengthened her own stride, easily catching up with him. "Let's hurry, I don't want to miss anything."

He ignored the way her shoulder brushed his. "I wouldn't worry about that if I were you. Ready usually means anywhere between five minutes and five hours."

"Well, if it's five minutes, you already wasted four of them with that nonsense at the truck. Why didn't you just tell me a foal was being born?" She jogged to the barn.

He let her run ahead, wondering if there was any way he could pull this off with her in one end of the barn and him in the other. Probably not.

By the time he'd gotten to the barn, Hank had already wandered up the wide cement aisle and introduced himself to Crissy. The old man's gnarled hand was closed over her small one and they were chatting easily.

If anyone could make Crissy feel welcome here, it was Hank. No one was better with people—or horses—than the wizened old cowboy.

Tate stepped up to them. "How's the mare doing, Hank?"

The old man let go of Crissy's hand and turned to him. "She's doing fine. I take it you're staying for the birth."

"Yep."

"Good. I'm taking my old bones back to bed then. With five more mares due this month, I'll take my sleep where I can get it. You know where I am if there's a problem."

Tate nodded.

"I'm off then." Hank turned to Crissy. "Nice to meet you, ma'am. You two have a good evening. And remember that old girl is eighteen, Tate. Don't make her do all the work herself."

"Don't worry, she's in good hands."

"I wouldn't be leaving her if she wasn't," he said good-naturedly, heading out of the barn.

Tate pulled the door shut, closing the night out. The sudden intimacy of the quiet barn hit him full force. A silent groan echoed through his head. Maybe bringing Crissy out here hadn't been the smartest decision.

Yes, it had been, dammit. She was excited about the foal. That's what her attention was on. And there was no reason her attention shouldn't stay there as long as he kept his hands to himself.

Tucking his hands back in his pockets, he headed down the aisle. "Come on, let's go see what's going on."

He walked down the aisle, way too aware of Crissy walking beside him, and stopped in front of the pregnant horse's stall. Peering in, he checked on the big sorrel.

She ambled restlessly in the straw-filled enclosure.

Crissy stepped up next to him and looked in. "She's pretty. What's her name?"

"Suzie. She's one of your dad's foundation mares."

"What does that mean? Foundation mare?"

The mare walked over to them, the expression in

her liquid brown eyes a little distressed, a little distracted.

"It means she's the mother, grandmother or great-grandmother to over half the horses on this ranch. Aren't you, girl?" He reached through the wire and scratched her nose.

The mare pushed harder against his fingers as if asking for a harder scratch, but then she turned away before he could deliver and paced restlessly to the other side of the stall.

Crissy winced. "She looks pretty uncomfortable."

"I imagine she is. See the way the veins are popping up under her skin along her neck and chest, and the sheen of sweat starting to darken her coat?"

"Yeah. What does it mean?"

"Means she's pretty far into labor. My guess is, it won't be long now."

Crissy shifted on her feet, the excitement obviously getting the better of her, but her brows crumpled with concern. "You don't give them drugs? Painkillers? So they're not so uncomfortable?"

"No. They're pretty much on their own."

She winced again. "Poor thing. I hope it goes quickly."

He liked the empathy Crissy had for the living things around her—despite the trouble it had caused at roundup the other day. He liked the way she looked out for those who couldn't look out for themselves. "It usually does with her. There's no reason to think this time will be any different."

Crissy's knuckles turned white as she gripped the

top board on the stall and peered through the mesh wire covering the upper half.

He smiled, watching her and remembering the first dozen times he'd seen a foal or calf born. He'd been both anxious and excited, too, the two emotions swirling around each other, feeding each other, turning the event into an exhilarating roller-coaster ride of worry and wonder.

Head down, Suzie grunted softly on the other side of the stall and a gush of liquid streamed from under her tail.

"Her water's breaking," he said. "We're on a short stick now."

Crissy gripped the board a little tighter. "I've never seen a birth before. What are we going to see first? Head, feet, butt?"

"If everything is going right, we'll see the front feet first."

She bounced on her feet, peering into the stall. "This is too cool."

He slanted her a look. "Just think how many babies you can welcome into the world if you stay."

She gave him a look of her own. "No lectures, Tex. Just let me enjoy the moment."

The mare grunted again, diverting both their attentions back to her. Her big, red sides heaved as a contraction hit her.

Crissy shifted anxiously. "Oh, geez, that cannot possibly feel good. Why doesn't she lay down? She's not going to have the baby standing up, is she?"

"Nope. She'll go down—"

As he spoke the mare folded her legs under her the best she could and lowered herself to the ground in an awkward move that sent straw flying.

"—any minute now." He smiled, watching the mare roll onto her side and stretch her legs and neck out. They would indeed be ushering a new foal into the world very soon.

Another contraction hit the mare. And then another just a couple of minutes later.

He shifted position, giving himself a better angle on what was happening in the stall. "Here we go. We've got hooves?" Not wanting her to miss a second, he pulled Crissy around in front of him. "See the little hooves. They're still covered by the birth sac, but if you look you can see them."

"I can see them." Awe sounded in her voice.

The feel of her body next to his sent a shock wave of need rocketing through him. Forcing his fingers to let go, he stepped back to a safer distance.

"How much longer?" she asked. "Didn't Hank say you should help her?"

"Once she's delivered the front legs, head and neck, I'll go in and help her with the shoulders. Right now, she not only doesn't need my help, she'd probably rather not have it."

Crissy wiggled with excitement and then held her breath as the mare pushed through another contraction.

He smiled. "We've got a nose."

"No kidding. Will you look at the size of those nostrils?"

He chuckled. "Horses are big animals. They need lots of oxygen."

The mare pushed again and they had a whole head. Despite the fact it was still enclosed in the sac, all the details were visible.

Crissy pointed at the emerging baby. "Look, it has a blaze."

He smiled. "A big ol' blaze. And two white socks." He shook his head. "It's going to be a gaudy thing."

She leaned closer to get a better look. "You're right. Socks. I totally missed those before. But he's not gaudy, he's *beautiful.*"

"He, huh?"

She nodded. "Absolutely. Look at that handsome face."

Tate would much rather look at Crissy. The soft blond curls swirling over her shoulders, the sexy line of her hip, the excitement sparkling in her eyes.

She looked at him, her brows knit in worry. "And speaking of his face, shouldn't you remove the sac from it? He can't breathe in there, can he?"

He forced his mind back to the duty at hand. "No, he can't breathe in there. But I don't want to remove the sac yet. Until the neck is delivered sometimes the foal slips back in. And you don't want him trying to breathe then."

"Oh, geez, I imagine not."

But a couple more pushes delivered the neck without incident.

"Okay, that's our cue."

Crissy looked back at him, her brows crashing together. "Our cue?"

"Yep. Time for you to deliver your first foal." He quietly stepped into the stall, leaving the door open for Crissy.

She stared at him, eyes wide. "You're kidding, right?"

"Absolutely not. This is your ranch. Your baby. Get in here and deliver him."

She swallowed hard. Wiped her hands down her jeans. "Are you sure?" Fear and anticipation sounded in her voice.

"Come on. I'll give you a hand."

The mare looked up as Crissy came into the stall.

Crissy held her hands in front of her. "Easy girl, I'm not going to hurt you." She raised worried eyes to his. "Am I?"

"No. You're going to help her."

She wiped her hands down her jeans again. "But I don't know what I'm doing."

"Well, you're doing great just the same. I want you to keep your movements slow, your voice calm, just like you're doing now. I'll help you with the rest."

"What do I do?"

"The next time the mare pushes, I want you to grab hold of the baby's front feet, sac and all, and pull gently downwards, towards Suzie's hooves. Got it?"

She nodded and moved into place, half crouching, prepared to grab the foal's feet. "What if I goof up?"

"You won't." He moved in behind her, prepared to

help if she needed it. "Give the mare a reassuring pat. Let her know you're here."

She did, her movements a little stiff, but her voice was calm as she said, "Easy girl."

Suzie grunted again and her big red sides heaved.

He gently nudged Crissy's shoulder. "You're on."

She reached for the baby's feet, her small hands wrapping around the foal's ankles, but her grip was light. Too light.

He rested a reassuring hand on her hip. "Don't be shy. Take a good strong hold. That membrane is tough. You can't hurt it. And at this stage of the game it wouldn't matter if you did."

She tightened her hold.

"Good. Now pull."

Her face a study in concentration, she pulled gently outwards.

"Down, remember. Toward the mare's hooves."

She adjusted the angle. But the baby barely moved.

"Pull harder. Don't waste this contraction."

She braced her feet and leaned back, her heart-shaped bottom leading the way. "I don't want to hurt him. Or her."

"You're not going to hurt either of them. Pull harder."

She leaned back more. But it wasn't going to be enough. Never having delivered a baby before, she was afraid to use as much muscle as required.

He was going to have to help.

Which was going to require he get a whole lot closer

than he was right now. He swallowed hard. Considering the way her butt was poking toward him, and the heat already curling through him, a risky proposition. But a riskier one was to stand here and do nothing. Let something go wrong with this birth. That he couldn't risk.

Gritting his teeth, he wrapped his body around hers, her butt snuggled into his lap, her back against his chest. He stretched his arms down beside hers and gripped the foal's legs just above her hands. "A little harder, Crissy." He added his strength to the task.

Following his lead, Crissy leaned back more, pulling harder.

He eased up, making sure the baby wasn't pulled too hard or fast for the mare and tried desperately not to notice Crissy's butt wiggling against him. Tried desperately not to think that sharing this moment with her was the best time he'd had in…forever.

Blocking both thoughts, he concentrated on the foal.

The shoulders slowly but surely slipped from the mare. Once they were out, the rest of the foal followed in a rush, its long back legs sliding free.

Tate let go of the baby and stepped away, drawing a deep stabilizing breath. But they still had work to do. "Okay, let's get that sac off him. We want him breathing now."

A hint of panic raced across Crissy's face. "How do I do that?"

"Just take a good hold of the sac with your hands

and tear." He demonstrated, wanting the foal to get oxygen as quickly as possible. "Now help me peel it off."

Crissy crouched beside him, her knee bumping his as she helped pull the tough, elastic material from the foal.

The small horse took its first breath, air rushing into his lungs and expanding his rib cage. Big, brown eyes blinked open.

"Amazing." The word was a bare whisper as Crissy stared at the wet, curly baby. "Look at him. He *is* beautiful." Wonder filled her expression.

Something inside Tate shifted, ached. What would it be like to share a life with this woman? To be the one to see that look on her face whenever she discovered something new and glorious?

God, he wanted her. With every fiber of his being.

His gut clenched. Mercilessly forcing his thoughts back to reality, he gently lifted the foal's back leg and peeked under. "You're right, it's a boy."

"Of course it's a boy. Just look at this face." She kneeled near the baby's nose.

The mare, still recovering from the birth, lay quietly on her side, regaining her strength. But the baby pulled its legs under itself, raised its head and poked his small nose at Crissy's knee.

Crissy laughed softly, rubbing the soft velvety end of his nose.

The baby leaned into it, his eyes closing to half-mast.

Tate chuckled. "Already getting spoiled."

"Hey, spoiling is good." She scratched behind the foal's ears, clearly in seventh heaven.

It was a moment he couldn't waste. "You stick around you can spend the rest of your life spoiling baby horses."

She raised her gaze to his. "You play so dirty, cowboy."

Ignoring the admonishment, he drove his point home. "There isn't anything that happened at roundup that can't be fixed."

She sighed, shaking her head, shadows scudding across her gaze. "Beyond the fact that half the cowboys on this ranch think I'm nuts or some evil city slicker sent here to make their lives miserable, I didn't like what I saw, Tex. I can't work somewhere where animals are being hurt."

"Then we won't hurt them. Branding has its advantages, but there are ways around it. For that matter, there are different ways to do almost everything on a ranch. If one method doesn't suit you, we'll find one that does. And if worse comes to worst, you can sell the cattle. Concentrate on horses." He tipped his head toward the colt.

She raised a brow. "How do I know there's not some horrible thing you do to horses here?"

He huffed in exasperation. "You're missing the point. If you stay, the Big T will be *your* ranch. If you don't like the way something is done, change it."

"Change it?" Surprise flashed in her eyes, but hesitation quickly chased it away. "From what you told me about my dad and his Santa Gertrudis, he'd probably turn over in his grave if I sold the cows."

"Cattle," he automatically corrected. "If you sold the *cattle*. But you're wrong about that. You're dad built this ranch because he wanted something wonderful to bring you and your mom home to. He did *not* build it as a shrine to himself. And if there are things you need to change to make this the home you always wanted, he would be the first to tell you to make them."

She stared at him, as if trying to decide if he were telling the truth or making it up. "You think?"

"I know."

She ran her hand down the foal's neck, her expression intense, thoughtful.

"Crissy, a lot of mistakes were made twenty-two years ago, by both your mother and father. But by and far the biggest one, in my opinion, was your mother walking away and never looking back. Never giving herself and your father the chance to make things right. From what you said, leaving at the first sign of trouble and never looking back was a habit of hers. Before you decide to walk away from the Big T, make sure this isn't one of your mother's traits you're glomming on to."

She stroked the colt's neck again, her brows crumpled in thought. "Do you think that's what I'm doing, giving up at the first sign of trouble?"

"Only you can answer that. But you might want to consider that maybe the reason you haven't found the job you want is because you give up too early on the ones you try."

Her hand stilled on the horse's neck.

He stayed quiet, letting her think it through.

Finally, she raised her gaze to his. "Maybe I have given up too early in the past. But…if I stay, you may not like the changes I make. And from what I saw at roundup, it's a damned safe bet a lot of the cowboys won't like them."

He'd managed to snag her attention. Now he had to reel her in. "Contrary to what you think you saw yesterday morning, the cowboys want you to stay, not go."

She shot him a yeah-right look. "I saw their faces, Tex. If they weren't looking at me like I was nuts, they were looking at me like they'd like nothing better than for me to drop off the face of the earth."

"You don't know any of those men well enough to know what they were thinking. Were they tense? Absolutely. They saw a woman who looked and acted like she wanted to shut the ranch down. The Big T is a big ranch; finding a buyer who can afford it all could take time. They know the chances of it being carved into smaller pieces to accommodate most buyers are good. They were undoubtedly worried about where they'd be sleeping in six months. But you let them know you want to keep the place going, even if it's in a different form, they'll bend over backwards to make you happy."

He could see the hope growing in her eyes. The resolution. She ran her fingers through the sparse hairs that made up the colt's mane. "Will you show me how to train him when he's old enough?"

"Absolutely."

A cautious smile started to push its way across her lips. "I think I'm going to name him Little Moe."

He chuckled. "Cute."

She looked up at him, white teeth gleaming. "I think so."

Suddenly, Suzie rolled up and pushed to her feet with an exhausted groan and a flurry of straw.

"That's our cue to get out of the way. Time for mama to take care of her baby." He pulled Crissy to her feet and guided her out of the stall.

Standing shoulder to shoulder in the aisle, they looked in, watching.

Suzie nuzzled the foal, checking him out, and then she went to work licking him clean. Little Moe's eyes closed in pleasure as mama cleaned his ears.

Crissy smiled at the maternal scene. "She's a good mom."

"The best. She'll be nudging him up for his first meal soon."

Crissy turned to him, her eyes shining. "I'm going to stay, Tex. And I'm not going to sell the cattle. No one else is going to heat a branding iron for those cute babies, either." She held her hand up. "I know they're a commodity. I know they're all eventually going to end up on somebody's plate. But until that day, they're going to live in paradise."

Triumph surged through him. "Not a problem. We'll work it out."

"Yeah, we will." She gave him an enthusiastic hug. But what started as innocent excitement quickly changed to something else.

The air around them heated.

Her eyelids dropped to half-mast. Her breathing quickened. Her smile turned seductive. "And now that I have that little detail taken care of… Let's move on to other things, shall we?"

His heart tripped.

She looked up at him with those sultry eyes and ran a finger down his jaw. "Kiss me, cowboy."

Oh, God. Every nerve in his body exploded. He needed to get out of here. Before things spiraled out of control. He'd done his job. He'd convinced her to stay. Now he needed to run.

But his feet didn't move.

Her knees bumped his. The soft plumpness of her breasts pressed against his chest. Her hand, soft and warm, cupped his face.

God help him. He wanted to kiss her. Wanted to taste the excitement shimmering through her. Wanted to pretend, if only for a moment, that he was a normal man with a mundane past and a bright future stretching before him.

But that wasn't the case. And pretending it was wouldn't be fair.

He closed his eyes and clenched his hands at his sides, resisting the urge to touch her by sheer force of will. He needed her to let go. Back off. Quit pressing her sweet little body against his. "Crissy—"

"Shh." She placed her finger over his lips. "Stop thinking about whatever lies beyond this moment, cowboy. I'm not asking for a profession of love or any big commitment or your firstborn child. I'm just asking for a kiss. One…" She leaned closer, her breath whispering over his cheeks. "Single…" Her arms slid around his neck. "Kiss." Her lips whispered over his.

His will snapped.

Chapter Nine

His lips closed over hers.

Hot.

Hard.

Greedy.

Crissy drank him in, drawing in a long, deep breath of his spicy aftershave. Running her hands over his strong, broad shoulders. Reveling in his kiss.

Breaking her moratorium on men the second she'd made the decision to stay on the Big T was maybe rushing things a bit. But…

He deepened the kiss, pulling her closer, slipping his tongue past her lips to taste and explore and claim.

Maybe it wasn't. No kiss had ever felt this hot or this urgent or this damned…erotic. The intensity with which he kissed her was frightening.

Exciting.

Intoxicating.

It was as if he wanted to devour her very soul.

Something that should have scared her to death. But it didn't. Beneath his hard core of determination was a gentle, caring heart. One that brought a bottle of tequila to soothe the turmoil of a difficult day. One that waited to show her a closet full of gifts until she could appreciate them. One that sent her roses as a gentle reminder of her dreams.

She wanted to know that heart better. Wanted to be closer to it. Closer to the man who owned it. She opened her mouth, letting his tongue in deeper, tasting his heat, his need.

His hands moved down her back, pulling her hips to his.

Yes. Electric tingles shot through her. He was so big and so strong and so damned hard…everywhere. With a soft groan, she pressed closer, reveling in the feel of him, reveling in the knowledge that he wanted her as much as she wanted him.

An answering groan vibrated from his lips, and the next thing she knew she was backed up against the rough wooden planks of the stall, one of his hands plowing through her hair, the other lifting her leg alongside his hips, opening her to him.

Oh, yeah. She rocked her hips forward, hot need slicing through her. She'd been attracted to him from the moment she'd first seen him. Had wondered more than once what it would be like between them.

But she'd never imagined anything like this.

This was explosive. Like throwing gasoline on a fire. She cursed the material separating them. She wanted to feel those supple muscles beneath her fingers. Wanted to feel his skin against hers.

Wanted to feel him, long and hard, inside her.

Now.

She slid her hands up his torso, loving every inch as she made her way to his collarbone. There, she grabbed hold of both sides of his shirt and pulled. The pearl-buttoned snaps gave way with one soft pop after the other.

His lips jerked away from hers. His whole body tensed. "Oh, God. What am I doing?"

No. No, no, *no*. She wasn't going to let him have some attack of conscience—or whatever the heck this was—now. She grabbed his shirt and held on tight. "You're kissing me. And I'm enjoying every second of it. Don't you dare stop."

He shook his head, his breathing hard and ragged. "We can't do this. *I* can't do this."

"But you *were* doing it. Really well, I might add." She didn't even try to keep the whine from her voice.

He let go of her leg, untangled her hands from his shirt and stepped back. "You're going to make a good home for yourself here, Crissy. A good life. But beyond my role as foreman of this ranch, I don't belong in that picture."

"What the heck do you mean, you don't belong in the picture? For pity's sake, if you hadn't been around to hold me up the last few days, I would have fallen apart by now."

"No, you wouldn't have. You're too strong for that. And supporting you through a tough time isn't the same thing as taking you to bed. Which is where that kiss was heading." He took another step back. "You need help with the ranch, I'm your man. You need anything else, you need to look elsewhere." He turned on his heel and started down the aisle.

She ran after him, grabbed his arm and pulled him back around. "Wait a minute. You can't kiss me like that and then just walk away."

He looked down at her, something cold and bleak and…immeasurably lonely filling his expression. "It's the only thing I can do." He pulled from her grasp and headed out of the barn, his boots ringing hollowly on the hard cement.

She watched him go, her lips throbbing, her body aching, her heart squeezing. "This isn't over, Tex."

He looked back at her as he pulled the big wooden door open and stepped into the night. "Yes, it is." He closed the door between them.

She narrowed her eyes on the long, marred planks. "Oh, no, it's not."

A few nights later, Tate pulled up to his house and got out of his truck. Every muscle and bone ached with fatigue. It had been a long brutal day at roundup. Tomorrow, which would be rolling around in another couple of short hours, would be another. Thank God.

He needed the work. Needed the exhaustion to keep the images of Crissy at bay.

Crissy looking at him with heat and need in her eyes.

Crissy in his arms, stretching toward him, rocking her hips into his.

Crissy—

"Hey, Tex."

He startled as he stepped onto his porch. Was he hearing her voice now? Great.

But when he peered into the shadows he spotted her sitting in his rocker, rocking. At least he wasn't crazy. But he was alone with her, here in the middle of night. And every nerve and cell in his body knew it. "What are you doing up so late?" He kept the question short and curt.

"Waiting for you." Her voice was as warm and sultry as the night air. "You've been avoiding me."

Hell, yes. And he had every intention of continuing to do so until this attraction between them died out. Considering the way that kiss had gone, a year—or ten—ought to do it. "Roundup is a busy time of year."

"I haven't noticed any other cowboy dragging his butt home after midnight."

"No one else is the foreman of this ranch."

"Ahh. So your long hours are strictly duty-related?"

"Of course."

"Hmm." She stared at him from the shadows. "I don't believe you."

"I can't help that."

She pushed up from the rocker and walked over to him. "I thought you were going to teach me how to train Little Moe."

He resisted the urge to reach out and touch her. Resisted the urge to pull her into his arms and pick up where he'd cut things off the other night. "He's only a few days old, Crissy. With the exception of halter training, which Hank can help you with, he won't need anything until he's two."

She peered up at him through thick lashes. "Is that how long you plan on avoiding me? Two years? Did the kiss scare you that much?"

It had scared the living daylights out of him. But having her here, obviously pursuing the matter, pursuing *him,* scared him more. He'd already proved he had no resistance where she was concerned. And the desire pounding through him now only underscored that truth.

He needed her to keep her distance, not come knocking at his door. "The kiss was a mistake. One I don't intend to repeat. Now, is there anything concerning the ranch I can help you with? If not, I'd like to get some sleep. I have a long day ahead of me tomorrow."

"Oh no, you are not going to shut me out that easily. We're going to talk about this. You're going to explain why you walked out on me."

He tightened his fist around his keys. If he told her, he wouldn't have to worry about keeping any distance between them. She'd be the one keeping it. But she might well decide to keep it by firing him. And he couldn't risk that. Not yet.

He'd convinced her to stay the other night. But he wasn't a fool—at least not about some things. He'd obviously been out of his mind when he'd kissed her, but he was clearheaded about this. She'd decided to stay, yes, but, considering her past record with jobs, that decision would be fragile at this stage of the game. He needed to stay around long enough to solidify it. Then, if she found out who he was, what he was and sent him packing…

In the meantime, he needed to shut this discussion down. "I'll take that as no, you don't have any questions about the ranch. In which case, good night." He slipped inside before she could stop him, bolted the door shut and walked away from it.

As far away from it as he could get. Far enough, he hoped, to keep him from jerking it open and pulling her in with him.

He made his way into the kitchen. If he drank himself into oblivion, maybe he wouldn't spend the night hot and agitated and miserable. He snatched an unopened bottle of tequila from the cabinet and broke the seal.

He could hope.

Chapter Ten

The next morning, Crissy headed down the stairs, her bare feet sinking into the thick carpeting. It had been another long, sleepless night.

Shaking her head, she wondered, for perhaps the millionth time, what McCade's deal was. Wondered what his cryptic remark about not belonging in the picture with her meant. Wondered why he was running the other way so fast when the chemistry between them was obviously so good.

She smiled ruefully. A few days ago she'd been glad of his reserve. Now, it was just frustrating. Unfortunately, she wouldn't be getting to the bottom of that little problem this morning. She'd seen the cowardly beast's truck disappearing across the field before the sun came up this morning. She'd have to snag him later.

In the meantime, there were other questions she needed answered. Questions about the ranch. She thought Braxton could help her with those, and she'd noticed his truck was still parked in the yard. Once she had her shoes on, she'd hunt him down.

She hit the bottom of the stairs and headed toward the kitchen, tennies in hand. The three pairs of socks she'd had with her when McCade had snagged her in Alaska were in the dryer.

She pushed through the swinging doors—to find Braxton leaning against the counter, eating a bowl of cereal.

"Hey," she said. "Thinking of the devil."

He looked up at her. "Looking for me?"

"I was gonna be as soon as I finished dressing."

He looked down at the tennies dangling from her fingers. "You need a pair of boots. If a horse or cow steps on your foot in those things you're going to be sorry. And on a ranch, sooner or later, something's going to step on your foot."

She looked at the tennies, taking in their soft construction. "You're probably right. But since I barely have enough money in savings to cover the rent on my place in Denver until I can get back there to collect my things, I don't think boots are in the budget."

"I've been meaning to talk to you about that. While you won't have access to any of your dad's money for the next six months, he did create a fund so you could pay your bills and have a little spending money during this time. He didn't want you to be out anything if you decided not to stay. There's plenty of money there to cover your rent."

"Great. Then boot shopping's back on. Is there a boot store nearby?"

"One in Casey's Gulch."

"That little town about ten miles down the highway?" she asked in disbelief. The place didn't look big enough to have more than the gas station that sat out on the highway.

He smiled, spooning up another bite of cereal. "Cowboys gotta dress, too. And they prefer to shop local. Tott's isn't as fancy as the city stores, but they stock the staples. Jeans, work shirts and a pretty wide selection of boots."

She zipped into the small laundry room connected to the kitchen as she talked. "Will they take an out-of-town check?"

"No need. I'll give you a signed check from the ranch. You can fill out the amount once you've picked out the boots—and whatever else you need. There's plenty of money in the fund, and I know Tate dragged you here on short notice."

She grabbed her socks from the dryer and strode back into the kitchen. "Fine, but I have a better idea than sending the check with me. Can they spare you from roundup today?"

"I imagine."

"Good. Then come with me to town. I have a ton of questions about the ranch. You can answer them while we drive. Then you can just write the check for the store."

"We can do that. But McCade is probably the best person to talk to about the Big T. As the foreman, he's involved with every aspect of the place."

"Don't worry, I have every intention of lassoing that boy later." Boy did she. "But what I'm interested in at the moment is the ranch's finances. That's your bailiwick, isn't it?"

He nodded.

"Good, then grab your hat and let's go."

Five minutes later, they were bouncing down the dirt road in Braxton's truck. "So what do you want to know?" he asked.

She chuckled. "I'm not exactly sure. Why don't we start with how much this place made last year. Maybe that'll give me an idea of what's possible and what's not."

"Last year, it cleared almost half a mil."

"Half a…" She stared wide-eyed at him. "The Big T sold half a million dollars in cows?"

"Cattle, Crissy. Cattle. And yes, a big chunk of the profit came from beef. But your father also has other investments and a stock portfolio. And the horses made good money last year. Very good money."

She took a deep breath and expelled it slowly. Cattle, horses, investments and stock portfolios? Maybe she should have taken her business classes more seriously. "Okay, this is more complicated than I thought. Let's take a different direction. McCade said Dad funneled most of his profits back into the ranch to grow it. But as far as I'm concerned, the Big T is plenty big enough. So I'm going to want to channel that money in a very different direction."

He cleared his throat. "Can I ask what you have in mind?"

"You know what the Alpine Angels do, right?"

"Fund-raisers for people in medical crisis."

"Right. And I want to use the profits the Big T makes to do more of the same."

His expression turned thoughtful. "Sounds interesting. And as long as you're careful not to cut into the money needed to run the ranch, you should have a steady source of income for the Angels. And there are some great tax benefits to that scenario."

Excitement skittered through her. "So you think it's doable?"

He nodded, obviously intrigued by the idea. "Absolutely. However, if your goal is to turn the Big T into the base for a charity organization, you might want to keep some of the money for growth. Because the bigger the Big T is, the more money it will make. And the more you can give away."

She thought about that for a sec. "Okay, you have a point. But making the Big T bigger might be a little tricky, since I'm not sure about the cattle. As you noticed at roundup the other day, I have some problems with how that end of the operation is being run. I'm going to make some changes. And some of those changes might cut into profits."

He thought for a second. "Then think about increasing the horse end of the business. Or go heavier into investments. Your dad used investments strictly as a way to diversify. So he'd have money coming in during the down years in the cattle industry. But you could use them more proactively."

"I like that idea. Except... I don't know anything about investing. Did Dad make his own investment decisions or did someone do it for him?"

"Your father always made the final decision, but I found the investments for him."

"Really? I thought you were just the bookkeeper."

He smiled. "I said I did the ranch's books, and I do. But I handled all your father's financial needs. My job description probably leans more toward financial adviser than bookkeeper."

"So you could help me restructure things for the charity and help me grow the investment end of the business?"

"Absolutely."

Excitement poured through her. What portion of last night she hadn't spent thinking about McCade's kiss, she'd spent wondering how to turn the Big T into a moneymaker for the Angels' charity. It was thrilling to hear it was doable. "Okay, let's get together soon and start working on strategies."

"Just wander into the office when you're ready and we'll get busy. But first, it's time to shop. We're here."

She'd been so engrossed in their talk she hadn't noticed they'd driven into the tiny town.

Braxton drove past a gas station, the post office and a bank before pulling into a space in front of a store with a big display window and a sign that read Tott's Apparel and Sundries.

Sundries? There was a word one didn't see too often these days. Smiling, Crissy got out of the truck and strolled over to the display window. Two mannequins, one male, one female, stood in frozen poses, each wearing a pair of stiff Wranglers, a pearl-snap western-cut shirt, black cowboy hats and two pairs of the fanciest alligator-skin boots she'd ever seen. She pointed to them as Braxton joined her on the sidewalk. "Those are cool."

He chuckled, shaking his head a little. "Pretty fancy for real work." He held the door open for her.

"Maybe." She strode past him into the store and looked around. Racks and shelves of jeans and shirts and other "sundries" were scattered around the front of the store. She headed toward the back where she spied a small open area with a few chairs and a wall full of shoes and boots.

Once there, she spotted the alligator-skin boots immediately. She picked one of them up, the alligator skin smooth and tough beneath her fingers. Absolutely the coolest boot she'd ever seen. She turned it over.

Her eyes popped wide and her jaw dropped. She held the boot up so the sole was visible to Braxton and pointed to the sticker. "Fifteen *hundred* dollars," she mouthed.

Smiling, Braxton walked over to her. "If you're really hooked on those, there's plenty of money in the fund for them."

She shook her head. "No way would I pay fifteen hundred dollars for a pair of boots. I have a list of people I could keep in the medications they need for a year with that kind of money." She set the boot down and picked up a simple, black one.

Braxton shook his head and took it from her hand. "Not those. They're cheap, but you'll have blisters on top of blisters by the time you break them in. And they won't last more than a year."

He set the boot back on its shelf and pointed to a few pair of boots clustered on a larger shelf. "Look at those. They're a little more expensive but they won't ruin your feet while you're breaking them in and you'll be able to wear them until the day you die."

And they weren't quite as plain as the black ones, either. She checked the price on a pair of brown, two-tone ones. Very affordable.

"Hey, Brax. You looking for new boots?" The young, female voice floated through the small shoe area.

Crissy looked up to see a pretty blond girl smiling broadly at Braxton, her big blue eyes filled with admiration. She squelched the smile that pulled at her own lips. She'd been right about Braxton turning cowgirls' heads. This one was obviously smitten.

"Actually, I brought Crissy in to buy." The smile Braxton gave the girl was polite and friendly but nothing more as he waved a hand toward Crissy. "Sue Ellen, I'd like you to meet Crissy Albreit, Warner's daughter. Crissy, this is Sue Ellen Maitland. She's been working here at Tott's for the last year. Her daddy owns the ranch to the west of the Big T."

Sue Ellen's expression brightened. "Hey, it's great to meet you. I heard they'd finally found you. I'm sorry they didn't find you before your dad passed away. But he'd be glad you're here now. He always wanted the ranch to go to you."

It was nice to hear from someone besides McCade that her father had wanted her here. Crissy bobbed her head. "Thanks."

Sue Ellen nodded at the boots in Crissy's hand. "You wanna try those?"

"You bet."

"You got it. Have a seat." Sue Ellen tipped her head toward the chairs and disappeared into the back.

A man in his late fifties or early sixties, with gray hair and deep lines around his eyes, wandered in while they waited. As he made his way to the wall of boots, he looked their way, his lips turning down as he spotted Braxton.

Before Crissy could ask what the man's problem was, Sue Ellen returned with two big boxes in her arms. "Okay, let's give these a try." She set the boxes on the floor, looking at Braxton as she opened the top one. "So how are things going out at the Second Chance?"

Crissy looked at Braxton, surprise running through her. "The Second Chance? Do you work on another ranch as well as the Big T?"

Sue Ellen laughed, slipping the boots on Crissy's

feet. "That's just what a lot of the folks around here call the Big T, being as how your daddy gave so many cowboys a second chance and all."

"A second chance?"

"Yeah, you know, cowboys down on their luck in one way or another, broke with no place to live or having little skirmishes with the law. A lot of folks around here wouldn't hire those men, but your daddy would if he had an opening. Even if he didn't sometimes. He thought everyone should have a second chance."

Something warm and fuzzy trickled through Crissy.

Sitting a few seats down, the old man snorted, the boot he'd picked to try on in his hand. "The Second Chance is only what the fools in these parts call your old man's place. The smarter ones call it the Little P." Pure contempt sounded in his voice.

"Shut up, Caldwell. Nobody asked for your input." Braxton spoke calmly, but the hard look in his eye made it clear he meant business.

The man curled his lips in a nasty sneer. "P, as in penitentiary. Half the men working on your dad's place are ex-cons. From thieves to drug dealers to murderers."

Murderers? She looked to Braxton, a cold chill swirling inside her.

"The man's jerking your chain, Crissy," Braxton quickly assured. "There are no murderers on the Big T."

The old man snorted again. "Just ask your foreman what he spent five years in Huntsville for, if you don't believe me."

She snapped her gaze to the man, the chill settling in her stomach. "The Big T's foreman?"

Pure hatred narrowed the man's cold, gray eyes. "That's right, your foreman, *Tate McCade*." He spat the words like bullets. And then, as if he couldn't contain his anger anymore and didn't want to do something he would regret, he slammed the boot he'd been holding on the chair next to him, thrust himself from his chair and stalked away.

She turned to Braxton, the chill spreading to her bones. "Is McCade an ex-con?"

"Let's talk in the truck." He nodded to the boots on her feet. "Those gonna work?"

How would she know? Her entire body was numb. "They're fine."

"Good, let's get out of here." Braxton grabbed her tennies and started stuffing them into the boot box.

Sue Ellen looked up at Braxton, her big blue eyes apologetic. "I'm sorry, Braxton. I—"

"Not your fault, Sue Ellen. It's not your job to control the local dissidents. Let's just get these rung up, shall we?" He crammed the lid on the box and helped Crissy to her feet.

A thousand questions pounded through her head as Braxton paid for the boots and escorted her back to his truck. Was this the reason behind McCade's reserve? The reason he'd left her standing in the barn that night, her lips throbbing, her body aching? And if it was, what then?

As soon as the truck was on the road she turned to

Braxton, her stomach tied in knots. "McCade's an ex-con?"

His lips pressed into a thin line he answered with a single nod.

Oh, God. "What did he do?"

Braxton shook his head. "Your father had a rule on the Big T. No gossiping behind people's backs. You want to know about someone, you ask him."

She couldn't believe her ears. "You're kidding, right? You're going to stonewall me? You don't think I have a right to know who's working on the Big T? You don't think I have a right to be a little nervous about the idea of living with a bunch of ex-cons?" She wanted to be PC about this. If the men were ex-cons, they'd paid their debt to society; she shouldn't penalize them with her prejudice. But the thought of living with a bunch of men who'd done God knew what was damned unsettling.

"Look, having made his own mistakes, your dad understood that sometimes people screw up. He didn't think they should pay their entire lives for it. But he wasn't an idiot, Crissy. He always hoped, always believed, he'd find you and your mother and bring you home. Do you really think he'd bring men onto the ranch who'd be a danger to you?"

"Quite frankly, I don't know what to think. But just because my father was comfortable with these men, just because he thought my mother and I would be safe around them, doesn't mean *I* will feel the same. I want to know who these men are and what they did. And I think I have that right."

He grimaced but nodded. "You're right, you do. But I won't talk behind their backs. What I can do is give you the names of the men with prison records. There aren't that many, by the way. Seven, to be exact. You can call them in, ask them yourself why they spent time behind bars. If they want to tell you what they did, fine. If not, you can decide if you want to let them go."

She stared out at the highway disappearing beneath the truck's hood, acid pouring into her stomach, a sharp ache throbbing suspiciously close to her heart. She thought she'd known what kind of man McCade was. Now she didn't have a clue.

But she was damned well going to find out.

She gave her head a sharp nod. "I can live with that. Let's start with McCade."

Chapter Eleven

Crissy paced anxiously behind her father's desk. The minute she and Braxton had gotten home she'd sent one of the hands out to lasso McCade, tell him he was expected back at the ranch. Pronto. She flexed her hands, trying to generate some warmth in her cold, clammy fingers.

Huntsville.

Texas's state penitentiary. The ominous title rang in her head, knotting her stomach and sending her feet skimming faster over the thick brown carpet.

Pain and anger slashed through her. She'd kissed him. And he'd kissed her back, dammit. How dare he not tell her he'd spent time in prison?

Two brisk knocks sounded on the door.

She spun to face the closed portal, squaring her

shoulders. If he even tried to avoid her questions, he was a dead man. "Come in."

The door swung open and McCade stepped into the office. "You wanted to talk to me?" His motions were stiff, his expression apprehensive.

He obviously sensed trouble. Smart man. Cocking up a toe, she pointed to her feet. "I went to town today and bought some boots. Like 'em?" She made no attempt to hide her anger.

He blinked fatalistically when she mentioned her trip to town. But he went through the motions of looking at her boots. "Very nice."

"Yeah, I kind of like 'em. But as it turned out, they weren't the highlight of the trip."

He raised his gaze to hers. "I'm not much for playing games, Crissy. Why don't you just get to the point?"

"I would have thought you liked games. You've certainly been playing them with me."

The corners of his lips turned down, but he didn't comment. He merely stood, waiting.

"Fine. No games. Why didn't you tell me you were an ex-con?"

He blinked and when he opened his eyes it was as if a light had been extinguished, as if his very soul had been blown out. "It's not something a man likes to advertise. Particularly if he's trying to gain someone's trust. And I needed you to trust me to get you on that plane in Alaska."

Ah, yes. His hard determination. The thing she'd

noticed first about him. Had he fooled her into thinking there was a softer side to him? "You've had plenty of opportunity since."

"Yes, I have. But things have been rather hectic since your arrival. And with all the emotions you were dealing with about your dad, I didn't think you needed more distractions."

She narrowed her gaze on him. "You didn't want me to know. Period."

He looked away. "No. I didn't."

Because of the reasons he'd just mentioned? Or because he didn't want her to think badly of him? Because her opinion of him mattered? "Well, now I know. What were you in for?"

He looked back, meeting her gaze squarely. "Attempted murder."

The breath rushed out of her. "Attempted…"

"Murder."

She fell back a step. "The man in the store hinted there were murderers living on this ranch, but…Braxton denied it."

"Because there aren't any murderers on this ranch. The charge was *attempted* murder. I didn't kill anyone. Though not for lack of trying." Anger vibrated in his voice, though at himself or the person he'd tried to kill she couldn't tell.

She ran a shaky hand through her hair, the world tilting beneath her feet.

He started toward her. "For crying out loud, sit down before you fall down."

She held her hand up, stopping him in his tracks. "I'm fine."

"You don't look fine. You look like you're about to pass out."

"I'm not going to make it that easy on you." She drew a fortifying breath and pulled her thoughts together. "Who did you try to murder?"

He grimaced, once again looking away. "A man."

"That's not an answer."

A muscle along his jaw flexed, but he said nothing.

She gritted her teeth. "Fine. A man. *Why* did you try to murder him?"

He gave her a sardonic look. "You think there's a good reason to take the law into your own hands? Trust me, there isn't."

Well, he seemed to have gotten that lesson down pat. But it wasn't the answer she was looking for. "*What* did this man do that made you want to kill him?"

More silence.

Anger sliced through her. "You know, McCade, you didn't cut me one ounce of slack when you dragged me across the country to this place. And I'm not cutting you any now. *Why did you try to kill that man?*"

He turned on her, anger and torment twisting his expression. "Because he raped my little sister."

"Your sister?" Confusion washed through her. "You told me you didn't have any brothers or sisters."

"I don't. Not anymore." The words were as bleak as the soulless look in his eyes.

"Oh, God. Did he kill her?" Her words were whisper thin, her anger slipping away.

"Not that day, he didn't."

Her stomach churned. "What does that mean?"

"It means Caldwell didn't kill her the day he raped her. Wasn't even around the day she died, but—"

"Caldwell?"

He nodded. "Evan Caldwell raped my sister."

"The man in Tott's this morning, the one who told me about the ex-cons working on the ranch, his name was Caldwell."

He grimaced. "That would be Evan's daddy. He's had a grudge against the Big T ever since I came to work here. Despite the fact I was in prison when they arrested his son and convicted him for another rape, he blames me for his boy's capture."

"If you were behind bars when his son was picked up, how can he blame you?"

"He blames me because I was the one who scarred Evan's face. And it was that scar that allowed his next victim to identify him."

"Next victim? He wasn't in jail for raping your sister?"

"He walked." McCade laughed, a cold, hollow sound. "Legal technicality."

More of her anger slid away, turning to empathy as his story unfolded. "That's why you went after him. Because the law wouldn't."

"I went after him because watching him walk the streets free as a bird after what he'd done to her was destroying Leanne."

"That was your sister's name? Leanne?"

He nodded, his eyes taking on a glassy look, as if he were gazing back over the years. "After the rape she was quiet, withdrawn. Pretty much what one would expect after a violent attack. But when Caldwell got off, she went nuts. Fighting with our folks, sneaking into bars, driving fast and pushing the envelope at every opportunity."

His words from the night she'd planned to go bungee jumping—the night he'd kissed her—echoed in her head. *It doesn't take a psychologist to know that anyone who flirts with the kind of danger the Alpine Angels rush into on a regular basis is fighting... something.* Her heart tripped. "You said Evan Caldwell wasn't around the day your sister died?"

"No." The single word was clipped, curt.

She didn't want to ask. She didn't want to think about a girl who'd been brutally raped. About a girl who'd seen her rapist walk free. But she had to know what had happened all those years ago. "How did she die?"

His expression was as cold as an arctic night. "Combined the drinking and fast driving one night. Drove her car off a cliff."

She closed her eyes. No wonder he was sensitive about the Angels' stunts. "I'm sorry."

"So am I." His eyes were as dull as his voice.

Her heart ached. For Leanne. For McCade. "Why did the charge end up being attempted murder instead of murder? Why didn't you kill Caldwell? Did you come to your senses, decide it wasn't worth it?"

"Oh, no, I wasn't that smart then. I fully intended to beat him to death. But Caldwell's neighbor saw me pull up, saw me pound my way through Caldwell's front door and he called 911. The cops didn't get there soon enough to keep me from doing some major damage to him, but they got there in time to save him."

Crissy couldn't imagine the rage that had sent him to that house. But she could sympathize with it. "I'm glad they got to you before you killed him."

"Why? Because you think he didn't deserve to die?" Anger vibrated in his voice.

She shook her head. "I think he probably did. But killing him yourself would only have ruined your life. I don't think that would have helped anyone. Least of all Leanne."

"No, it didn't help Leanne a bit."

She suspected there was more behind that remark than met the eye, but right now she needed to concentrate on the McCade part of the story. "How long were you in prison?"

"Five years."

And the anguish of every one of those years was evident in his eyes. "That's a long time."

"You can't imagine."

"No, I can't." She watched him quietly. "Is that why you walked away from me the other night? Because you're an ex-con?" She could see the shame that title caused him. "Is that what you meant when you said you didn't belong in the picture with me?"

"Oh, for crying out loud, Crissy, don't look at me like it *doesn't* make me the last kind of man you should have in your life."

She'd had McCade dragged in here because she'd wanted to know what kind of man he was. Wanted to know if he was the honorable, caring man she thought he was. Or a cold calculating criminal.

The regret she saw in his face for the decision he'd made all those years ago, the pain still haunting him for his sister's rape and death told her everything she needed to know. "I'm not sure it does. Going after Caldwell was stupid. But you did it for all the right reasons. How old were you when it happened?"

Impatience and self-deprecating anger snapped in his eyes. "Old enough to know better. And don't glorify or justify what I did. There's no justification for it. It was a stupid, irresponsible, *wrong* thing to do."

"Words spoken by an older, wiser man." A man whose life was unalterably changed by the events of a sad, tragic time.

"Wiser or not, I guarantee the only thing people see when they look at me is an ex-con. Scum of the earth. What I've done since prison doesn't mean a damned thing to them. And any woman whose name is attached with mine will be lowered to the same level."

"That's a little dramatic, don't you think?"

"Not a bit. Old man Caldwell might well have a personal beef with me, but I guarantee there are plenty of other people in town who view me and the other ex-cons on this ranch with the same contempt and loathing he does."

"I'm sure there are. Bigots have always been, and will always be, around. But there are also fair-minded people. People like Sue Ellen. She made it clear she had no qualms about the Big T. Or any of the men on it. And my father obviously thought a man's character was made up of more than his past mistakes. As for myself, I prefer to make up my own mind about a person."

His expression shuttered. "By all means, make up your own mind. But I'm not going to drag any woman down to my level. Least of all Warner's daughter."

"And I don't get any say in this?" Frustration pounded through her. "I'm supposed to ignore the fact that I still can't stop thinking about that kiss? That every time I'm around you, my nerves hum and little tingles race through my body?"

Tate's expression remained cold, detached. "Unless you're into frustration, I recommend that's exactly what you do. I have no intention of compounding the mistake I made thirteen years ago. I screwed up and I'll pay the price, but I'm damned well not going to let you pay it with me." He spun on his heel and strode out of the office, pulling the door closed behind him.

She plowed her fingers through her hair. She'd convinced herself McCade was the honorable, caring man she'd thought him to be. Convinced herself he was exactly the kind of man she wanted in her life. But convincing *him* was obviously not going to be so easy.

Chapter Twelve

Tate crouched by the rear tire of his truck, still cursing as he cranked the last nut on the lugs as quickly as he could. The sun had peeked over the horizon a good half hour ago. He needed to get this tire changed and get out of here before—

The front door of the big house creaked.

Damn. He hadn't been quick enough.

Footsteps echoed on the porch. He didn't bother to look over his shoulder. He knew who the footsteps belonged to. Knew where they were heading.

He swore as he set the crowbar aside and started lifting the tire from the rear axle.

The footsteps crossed the drive and stopped beside him.

"Hey, Tex."

He tossed the tire aside and narrowed his gaze at Crissy from his crouched position. "Slitting tires is pretty low, don't you think?"

She shrugged, taking another sip of coffee from the mug she cradled in her hands. "I did think about just letting the air out, but I was afraid you'd fix that too fast and be on your way before I could catch you. You're getting pretty good at this avoiding-me thing."

Apparently, not good enough. He straightened to his full height. "We're in the middle of roundup, remember? I have work to do."

"Braxton said the last of the cows—excuse me, *cattle*—were driven back to the open pastures two days ago. That sounds like roundup's over to me."

Note to himself: strangle Brax next time he saw him. In the meantime, he might need a more direct approach. "Maybe I think we could both use a cooling-off period."

She looked up at him through her lashes. "Maybe I don't want to cool off."

Desire slammed through him, hot and hard. Gritting his teeth, he turned away from her and strode to the tailgate. "We've already been over this."

"*You've* been over it. I don't recall you letting me have much say in the matter."

"That's because there isn't anything to say."

"Oh, there's plenty to say. Like, I think what's important is who you are today, not who you were all those years ago. And I like who you are today. I like the honor and quiet determination that make up the core of you. I like the way you watch out for me. And—" she shot him a sexy smile "—I like the way you kiss me."

And he liked the way she kissed back. Too damned much. "You're romanticizing a bit. Honor and determination." He snorted with contempt. "For crying out loud, I'm a cowboy doing my job. End of story."

"I'm not romanticizing anything. I've given this serious thought, and—"

"If you've thought about it and still think getting involved with an ex-con makes an ounce of sense, you're either very naive or not thinking as seriously as you should." He pulled the spare out of the truck's bed and went to work putting it on.

She sighed. "You know, if you weren't so damned honorable and determined, you wouldn't be fighting me on this. And I did give it serious thought. Getting involved with a man isn't something I take lightly anymore. In fact, I declared a moratorium on men after I left Tom. I thought if I was going to figure out what I wanted in life, it was best not to have any distractions while I did it."

So that's why she'd kept her distance in the beginning. He'd wondered. "A moratorium sounds like a good idea to me. I'd think twice before abandoning it."

"Oh, I did. But, thanks to your help—" she tossed him a cheeky grin "— I know what I want. I want to make the Big T my home and use it as a financial base for the Angels' charity. So you see, I don't need the moratorium anymore."

"If you don't show better judgment than you are right now, you need it more than you think." He put the last nut on the lugs, grabbed the tire iron and started tightening them, doing his best to pretend she wasn't there. Doing his best to ignore the aching need gnawing at his gut.

"Man, you're stubborn."

Not stubborn. Determined. Determined to give her everything Warner had wanted for her. Everything good and wonderful and bright. But that determination was weakening by the second. He needed to do what he'd been trying to do all week. Put some distance between them. "Don't you have things you need to be doing?"

"Actually, I don't. Certainly not anything as fun as this. Do you have any idea how sexy you look changing that tire?"

He lunged out of his crouch and closed the distance between them in two quick strides. "Stop it. Just stop it."

She smiled. "Why? Because—"

"Because teasing is only going to make this harder for us. And it's not going to get you what you want."

Her gaze, warm and knowing, skated over him. "I'm thinking it might get me exactly what I want."

The sound of a car horn tooting twice broke through her words.

They both turned, looking for the source of the disturbance. A car, its headlights still shining in the early morning light, was moving along the road that led in from the highway.

She looked back to him. "One of the hands coming early?"

He shook his head. "I don't recognize the car." But he was damned glad for its arrival. Two more seconds of her teasing and he'd have been tempted to strangle her. And God knew where that would have led.

The car drove down the road that snaked between the paddocks, heading toward them. Suddenly, blond heads were poking out of every window. Shrieks and hollers and hey-Crissys split the early morning quiet.

Crissy turned back to him with a wry smile. "Take a deep breath, cowboy. You've got a temporary reprieve. The Alpine Angels have arrived."

Thank God. Not just for the moment, but for the buffer they would offer for however long they stayed. "Did you know they were coming?"

She shook her head. "I've been talking to them about things on the phone since I came. They said they'd be coming eventually, but I didn't expect them this soon."

Things? He wondered uncomfortably if he was one of those things.

The car pulled to a stop, the girls piled out and then there was nothing but hugs and how-are-yas. Eventually Crissy took a step back. "Ladies, I'd like you to meet the foreman of the Big T, Tate McCade. Tate, this is Mattie, Josie and Nell." She pointed to each girl as she introduced her.

Despite the fact that they were all blond and very close to the same age, Tate noted they were easy to tell apart. Mattie was tall and statuesque. Nell was tiny, a flat five-foot-nothing with the frame of a humming-bird. And Josie, well, Josie was all curves and raw sex-uality. Not his type, but he imagined she attracted men like honey attracted flies.

He shook their hands and gave them polite nods. "Welcome to the Big T."

Their looks were sharp and knowing as they gave him the once-over.

Great. So much for wondering if he was one of the things Crissy had discussed with them. He obviously was. Which did not bode well. He was having enough trouble with Crissy without adding three more schem-ing females to the mix.

"You guys hungry?" Crissy asked. "We can go in and I'll cook you breakfast."

"That sounds great," Mattie said. "Then after break-fast, you can show us around the ranch. I can't wait to see the horses. Then tonight, we can put our party dresses on and go dancing. We spotted a place called Jimmy's Honky Tonk not too far down the road. Looks like a place that knows how to dish out fun."

Tate nearly choked. Crissy at the local meat mar-ket? He didn't like the sound of that one bit. "Jimmy's can get pretty wild. You might want to just stay in, rent a movie. The gas station in Casey's Gulch keeps a fairly current selection."

Josie laughed. "Wild is the Angels' middle name, cowboy. Of course, you could come, help keep us out of trouble." Pure calculation sparkled in her eyes.

They hadn't been here five minutes and they were plotting already. "Sorry. I have business here."

The curvy blonde just shrugged and smiled. "Too bad, it ought to be fun." She turned to Crissy. "I brought plenty of let's-go-dancing, turn-the-boys'-heads clothes. Perfect for a little celebration to kiss your moratorium on men goodbye."

Crissy looked to him, her green-eyed gaze locking on to his in challenge.

Just the thought of Crissy in another man's arms made him crazy. But he couldn't let himself be sucked into the girls' machinations. If he snuggled up to Crissy on a dance floor, it would all be over. They'd be in bed before the night was through. Not an option. He looked away, refusing to even play the game.

"Jimmy's it is," Crissy finally said, a definite edge to her voice. "Drinking, dancing and good-looking cowboys. Sounds like a good time to me."

They strolled off toward the house, arm in arm, chatting and giggling.

He stared after them, trying to pull air into his lungs. Crissy was not going to that bar looking for a man. She was just trying to make him jealous.

And, damn her sweet, curvy little hide, it was working.

"This is Pillar Creek." Crissy pulled her horse to a stop on the same small bunch of rock outcroppings McCade had shown her the valley from. She and the girls were killing the afternoon by touring the ranch.

At least the places Crissy knew how to get out to and back from without getting lost.

"It's beautiful," Nell said, stopping her horse next to Crissy's.

"Well, look who's come to join us." Mattie pointed down the road, a sly smile turning her lips.

Crissy turned to see McCade trotting down the road. "Well, that's a surprise." Considering the way he'd been avoiding her, he was the last person she expected to see.

He trotted up to them, tipped his hat. "Ladies."

Crissy lifted a single brow. "You lost, Tex?"

He smiled. "Nope. Hank said he'd saddled horses so you could show the girls around the ranch. I thought you might appreciate a tour guide."

"Well, that was nice of you." Josie gave him a big smile. "And you came just in time to see our race."

"Race?" Surprise flashed across Nell's face.

Crissy wanted to groan out loud at the obvious ploy to leave her and McCade alone. But she didn't waste her breath. Josie was incorrigible when it came to men and matchmaking. And besides, she could use the time alone with McCade to push her case. Make him see how stubborn he was being.

"Yes, our race," Josie said conspiratorially. "We're running over that mesa top and down to that tree on the far side. Everyone except Crissy, of course. She's judging, remember?"

"That's right," Nell agreed, quickly catching on.

"If you ladies haven't ridden any more than Crissy,

you might want to keep your race on the road. We'll be less likely to have to pick you up out of the dirt that way."

Josie waved away his concern. "We'll be fine. This is tame compared to the stuff we're usually doing."

"Which does not make me feel any better." He grimaced, looking over the race course. "You're going to want to be careful on the sides of that mesa or someone could take a nasty fall."

"Not a problem. Come on, ladies." Josie pulled her horse off to the side and brought him to a halt, creating the starting point for their race.

The other girls joined her, Josie hollered go and they were off, hooves and dust flying.

McCade turned to Crissy as they thundered away. "They're as subtle as a swarm of locusts."

Crissy laughed. "Yes, but they have gentler hearts." She watched the three horses fly toward the small flat-topped hill. "So, you want to tell me why you really came out here?"

He tipped a shoulder. "Four daredevils, four horses. I was afraid the four of you would cook up something that would get both you and horses killed."

She rolled her eyes. "So you came along to save us from ourselves."

"Something like that," he admittedly dryly.

"Oh, come on, we're not that bad."

He pointed toward the racing trio. "You're that bad. Do any of you ever stop to think about the consequences of your actions?"

She sighed, knowing how he felt about the dare-devil stuff. "You think we're like your sister, don't you? Troubled girls looking for a way to self-destruct?"

He just looked at her. But she knew what that look meant.

"I don't think we are. Which is not to say the extreme sports don't fill some need for each of us. I'm sure they do."

His gaze locked onto hers. "What need do they fill for you?"

"I don't know. Triumph maybe. Excitement surely."

"That's a pretty sketchy answer."

"That's because you're looking for some deep dark motivation. There isn't one. My mom was pretty sick by the time I was fifteen. I was doing everything I could to hold our world together. But I knew it was falling apart fast. Knew I wasn't going to be able to save it. I could, however, take my snowboard, one I'd picked up in a garage sale for five bucks, onto a mountain and conquer its slopes, no matter how tough they were. It was a small victory, but it was a victory—and I didn't have many of those back then. It was also fun and exciting, two elements that were almost nonexistent in my life. It was a good release. End of story."

"It means more to you than that, or you wouldn't still be doing it."

She laughed. "Well, it's still a good release. It's not like my life has been all that great in recent years, either. Remember, creepy boyfriends, dead-end jobs, college classes I don't care about. And beyond that, the backcountry snowboarding, which has made up the biggest portion of the Angel events, has allowed me to do the one thing in life that really matters to me. Raise money for people in medical crisis."

"Yes, it has. And since you've avoided killing yourself up until now, I'd say good for it. But now you have the Big T. Putting yourself at risk isn't necessary anymore."

She'd never thought of the risks she was taking in the past. When she was younger, the snowboarding had been fun—and she'd thought she was invincible. A few accidents and broken bones in her early twenties had taught her that wasn't the case, but then the idea of the charity came to her and putting herself at risk seemed acceptable when she looked at the end result. Particularly since she didn't really have much to lose.

But now she had the Big T and an opportunity to make a difference in more than a few people's lives. And, of course, there was McCade. "I'll think about it."

"You do that. And if those ladies mean anything to you, you might want to keep them in mind while you do it. Because sooner or later, the odds always catch up with you."

She watched the girls race their horses across the top of the mesa, heading for the inevitable trek downward, a frisson of alarm running through her. She'd been damned lucky to run into these women. They'd all added important things to her life. Wonderful things. The thought of anything happening to them…

She held her breath as the horses careered down the mesa's side, the girls rocking wildly in the saddles. When they finally hit the bottom of the mesa, all still on their horses, she breathed a sigh of relief. "So maybe I'll scale things back for future events. Maybe figure out a way to use the Big T. Not just as a financial base, but as place to run the events. I'll have to think about it."

He shot her a knowing look. "Good friends, huh? Might want to hang on to them for a while?"

She smiled, watching the girls streak by the finish line and pull their horses back to a walk. "The best. And now that we've solved the Angels' idiosyncrasies, let's take a closer look at yours, shall we?"

His expression turned dark. "I don't have any idiosyncrasies. I have a code of ethics that won't let me drag you into my mess. Looking at it closer won't change anything."

"Let's give it a shot, anyway."

"Let's not." He pointed to the girls. "Those horses are spent. They need to be *walked* straight back to the barn and put away. And since you seem to have finally grasped—at least in a fledgling manner—the idea of caution, my work here is done. I have to get back to my real job." Without another word, he turned his horse and galloped away.

Crissy stared after him, irritation pounding through her. She'd had him in her grasp and let him slip away.

Man, she hoped she had better luck tonight.

Chapter Thirteen

"**Y**ou look great." Mattie brushed one more of Crissy's curls into place and stepped back.

Josie tweaked the ruffles at Crissy's cleavage. "Oh, yeah, he sees you in this, no way he's going to let you trundle off to Jimmy's alone. If he lets you trundle off at all."

Crissy looked in the cheval mirror. With a trip into Tott's and a few things that had come out of her bag, Josie had worked miracles. Crissy was wearing a dark green, midcalf skirt, the crinkly, gauzy kind that had tons of material in it. It floated around the curve of her hips and swished softly, coyly, against her calves. With the flat, strappy sandals she wore, it represented the soft, feminine side of the outfit.

The strapless bustier top that nipped in her waist

and lifted her breasts like twin gifts to the gods was the leave-no-man-standing side of the outfit. Its white cotton eyelet material played peekaboo with her tanned skin, while the small ruffled edge that ran along the top drew a man's eye directly to her provocatively plumped breasts.

She frowned at her reflection. "I'm not sure about this. It feels…dishonest."

Josie tsked, fluffing her own curls in the mirror. "There's nothing dishonest about making a recalcitrant man sit up and take notice. Nor is there anything wrong with reminding him he isn't the only fish in the sea. Or in this instance, the only cowboy in Texas."

"He might not be the only cowboy in the state, but he's the only one I'm interested in. And—"

"And you said you've tried everything to pin the man down in the last week—to no avail," Mattie pointed out.

"That's true. But still—"

"But still, nothing," Josie admonished. "Relax, will you? You aren't committing a cardinal sin here. All you're trying to do is make the man come to you long enough for you to have a real conversation, right? Long enough for you to convince him he's being overly sensitive about this ex-con thing, right?"

"Yes. But—"

"But nothing. Do you want him or not?" Josie asked impatiently.

She did want him. And he wanted her, dang it. He was just too wrapped up in his skewed sense of honor to take her. Which meant it was up to her to make him see how wrongheaded he was being. She squared her shoulders. "I want him."

"Then let's go." Josie waved a hand toward the bedroom door.

They headed down the stairs, Crissy's stomach tied in a tight, aching knot. "What if this doesn't work? What if he doesn't come out of his house?"

"I saw his face when we mentioned dancing," Mattie said. "He'll come out. And if he doesn't, we'll go dancing."

God, Crissy hoped he came out. If he didn't, the last thing she was going to feel like doing was dancing.

They made their way onto the porch, Mattie and Josie talking and laughing in an animated fashion. Josie turned to her. "For pity's sake, girl. Smile, laugh, make him think you can't wait to get to the bar and start reeling in hunky cowboys."

Crissy forced a smile to her lips and managed a half-hearted giggle. But she was afraid the effort was futile. McCade's truck was parked in front of his house, but the house was dark. "I don't think he's home."

Josie threw a covert glance in that direction. "His truck's there."

"Yeah, but this is a ranch. Lots of horses available. He could very well be out checking on the cattle."

But Josie wasn't fazed. "He could just as easily be hiding in the dark, watching. Come on."

They chatted in front of the girls' rental car for a few minutes. But nothing at McCade's moved.

Crissy sighed, disappointment crashing over her. "If he's in that house, he's not coming out. You guys go on to the honky-tonk. I'm going back inside."

Josie grabbed her arm. "No, you're not. You're going with us. If he is in that house, watching, hoping you won't go at the last minute, we're calling his bluff. I bet he shows up at the bar by ten."

Crissy didn't hold out much hope for Josie's scenario. McCade had already told her he wasn't much for games. She was pretty sure he wasn't going to fall for this one. But the girls were looking forward to a fun night of dancing, so she crawled into the sedan, the night stretching out long and gloomy before her.

Tate urged Cutter up the hill, the hot Texas air surrounding him. The night was quiet. The moon full. The countryside peaceful. A late-night bareback ride usually calmed him.

But not tonight.

A river of acid poured through his gut. His chest felt like several strands of barbed wire were cutting it in half. And no matter how fast he and Cutter chased over the Texas terrain, he couldn't get the picture of Crissy out of his head.

When she'd stepped out of the big house tonight with the other girls, he'd just about had a heart attack. What the hell had she been thinking, putting on something that made her look as sexy as that top had? Every man at the honky-tonk would be drooling over her. He sure as hell had been, standing in his house in the dark, hiding so Crissy wouldn't see him spying on her. And the thought of some other cowboy drooling over her sent a white-hot surge of rage through him. It had taken every ounce of his willpower not to stalk across the road, toss her over his shoulder and lock her in the nearest closet. Or drag her to his bed.

Unfortunately, he couldn't do either. Not unless he wanted to pull Crissy down to his level. So he'd gritted his teeth and watched her crawl into the car with her friends and drive off to Jimmy's. A bar he knew would be filled with music, booze and horny cowboys.

Cowboys who wouldn't know she wasn't dressed for them.

He swore into the night. She might not be dressed for them tonight, but sooner or later she would be. Sooner or later she'd go home with one of them. Or bring one of them home with her. Sooner or later another man would kiss her. Take her.

He swore again, long and hard, as he pulled Cutter to a stop on the top of the small hill. He fully intended to sit here, all night if necessary, and wait for Crissy and the girls to come home. Stupid and sophomoric, like driving by a girl's house to see if she was there, but here he was.

The moonlight washed everything in a quiet, silvery light, making it easy to see the lone figure walking down the wide, dirt road. He squinted into the twilight. "Crissy?"

The figure startled, a surprised squeal bursting from

her lips as she looked up the hill toward him. But once she spotted him, she relaxed a bit. "Tex?"

He nodded, nudging Cutter down the hill, taking in her long, flowing skirt and that gravity-defying top. "What are you doing walking out here?"

Her lips twisted ruefully and she waved a hand down the road. "Here's a little bit of irony for you. I got a flat."

He smiled, relief flowing through him. It wasn't much past ten; if they were heading home this early, they obviously weren't having much fun romancing the cowboys. "I can fix that for you. How far back is the car? I take it the other girls are there, waiting for you to bring help."

She shook her head. "They were having too much fun at Jimmy's. They were going to close the place, then hitch home with some of the Big T cowboys there. And if the tire were fixable, I'd have done it by now. But the spare was flat, too."

He looked at her feet. The pretty leather sandals looked new. She probably had blisters on top of blisters already. He could hardly leave her here to finish the walk home. Although with the full moon overhead, only one horse to share and his nerves already drawn tighter than a lasso's noose, it would undoubtedly be the safer decision. Steeling himself for the ride ahead, he swung off the horse. "You can call the rental company in the morning. They can send someone to get it. In the meantime, let's get you home."

Her brows went up as she gave the horse a good look. "No saddle?"

"Not tonight. But that won't be a problem. Actually, considering your skirt, it'll make things easier." He lifted her onto the horse, sidesaddle fashion, both legs hanging off one side of the horse.

"Yikes." She grabbed Cutter's mane to keep her balance. "I'm not sure I can stay on this way once he starts moving."

"Don't worry, I won't let you fall." And putting her on astride would require rucking her skirt halfway up her legs. A display he was pretty damned sure he wasn't up to. He swung up behind her, settling her safely between his arms as he picked up the horse's reins.

The curve of her hip fit into his lap. The soft cushion of her breasts rested on his arm.

He gritted his teeth. Okay, this was every bit as bad as he'd imagined. And then some. But there wasn't much he could do about it, except do the best he could to keep his mind otherwise occupied. He pushed Cutter into a walk. "So how come you left Jimmy's early?" Despite himself, he wanted to hear that she hadn't found anyone who interested her as much as he did.

She grimaced, shifting on the horse to find her balance. "I wasn't having much fun, and there was this guy there, Bret Taverson. Know him?"

He blocked out the feel of her hip snuggling into his lap and tried not to notice that her perfectly plumped breasts were only inches from his gaze. His hands. His mouth. "Yeah——" Great, he sounded like he had a ton of gravel in his throat. He cleared it. "He works over on Carlson's spread. Although Bret tends to spend more time at the honky-tonk than he does working. Considers himself quite a ladies' man."

"No kidding. He was all over me." She shuddered. "The guy must have ten hands. And he kisses like a leech."

Shock ran through him. "You *kissed* him?"

She bristled indignantly. "He kissed *me*. And don't take that tone with me. If you didn't want other cowboys kissing me you should have come when we invited you."

His brows shot toward his hatband. "Let me get this straight. I wouldn't play, so you went looking for the first guy who would?"

"No," she snapped, her expression turning downright peevish. "But if I had, you couldn't possibly complain about it."

"The hell I couldn't."

Her gaze snapped to his, her eyes going wide and then narrowing to sly, green slits.

Dammit, he'd blown it now.

Her expression turned positively wicked. "What's wrong, cowboy? Did it bother you thinking I was at a bar with other men? Men who, unlike you, would have no qualms about dragging me down to their level?"

He looked away, refusing to take the bait. "Let it go, Crissy."

But it didn't take more than a glance at her sly expression to know she had no intention of letting it go.

"Ya know—" her voice dripped with saccharine innuendo "—Taverson wasn't really my type. But there were a lot of other cute cowboys there."

He pictured her checking out the cowboys at the bar. Pictured them checking her out. He drew a deep breath, reining in his jealousy.

"Josie pointed out this one guy who was giving us the eye. He was pretty cute, all dressed up in his Saturday-night best, with his dark, wavy hair and these rather startling gray eyes."

"Shut up, Crissy." He'd just spent the last three hours thinking about how much he wanted her, aching with that want. No way could he sit here calmly and listen to her talk about other men.

But she didn't even pause. "His shoulders weren't as broad as yours, but the rest of him wasn't bad. Great—"

His control snapped.

The day would surely come when he had to watch her walk into another man's arms. But, by God, today would not be that day. He slammed his lips over hers.

She didn't hesitate. She leaned into him, wrapped her arms around his neck and opened her mouth to his.

He deepened the kiss. She tasted hotter than he remembered. Sweeter. And he couldn't get enough. He pulled her closer.

Somewhere in the remotest part of his brain, he knew he was making a huge mistake. Knew he had no right to touch her. But no one knew they were here. No one would ever know what happened here under the moonlight. And he couldn't stop himself. He had to touch her. Had to taste her. Had to have her. Now, if not forever.

She pressed closer, shifting on the horse so she was turned more toward him.

Had anything ever felt this good? He cupped her breast, her soft fullness filling his palm. But a touch wasn't enough. He pulled his lips from hers. "I want to see you."

A slight blush colored her cheeks, but she made no move to stop him when he lifted her breasts from the skimpy, strapless top. The moonlight glinted off her, shimmering through the curls cascading over her shoulders, shadowing the space between her breasts and highlighting the full luscious globes and her pebble-hard nipples. He sucked in a hissing breath. "Gorgeous."

Desire darkened her eyes, and she reached for his shirt. "Let's level the playing field, shall we?" She pulled the plackets of his shirt apart, the sound of popping snaps reverberating around them as she bared his chest. She ran her hands up, starting at the bottom of his ribs and progressing up over his pecs. "Gorgeous doesn't cover it."

The fit of his jeans became downright painful at her look of admiration. He wanted to pull her off the horse and take her right then and there. But he resisted the urge.

This was a stolen moment. There would be no repeats of what happened tonight. He wanted it to be special. He wanted to be able to look back and remember every second. He wanted Crissy to remember every second. A hard, quick roll in the Texas brush didn't qualify.

Ruthlessly ignoring the need pounding through him, he pushed a curl back from her face and ran his finger over her delicate collarbone, savoring the silkiness of her skin, memorizing the delicate lines of her neck and shoulders and the seductive swell of her breasts. "Open country, a good horse and a half-naked woman. Every cowboy's dream."

"I don't want to be a dream. I want to be real. And I want this to go on. Every night." Her sultry voice floated through the warm Texas night. "Every second of every day."

His heart squeezed. "Shh. Just because you want something doesn't make it possible. Tonight is what we have. Let's not spoil it."

Pain flashed in her eyes. "I'm not going to spoil it, but I'm not going to give in to your martyrdom, either. I want more than tonight and I'm going to do everything in my power to convince you that you do, too." She pulled his lips back to hers.

He drank her in, savoring her taste, her heat. It wasn't about what he wanted. It was about what was best for her. But he wouldn't waste another moment arguing about it. Not tonight. He ran his hands up her back into the silky mass of her hair, angling her head just so.

She opened her mouth wider, allowing him deeper

access, her tongue sparring with his as she shifted on the horse trying to get closer. A frustrated sound vibrated in her throat, and she broke the kiss. "Let's get off the horse."

"I have a better idea." He pulled Cutter to a stop and with a few quick adjustments had Crissy straddling the horse backwards, so she was facing him, her legs over his, the very core of her snuggled up tight against his aching need, her hair streaming down her back, her skirt spread wide over her legs and his lap.

Her eyes went wide and then she chuckled, low and sexy. "You're a wicked man, Tate McCade."

He liked the sound of his name on her lips. Far, far more than he should. Pushing the thought away, he concentrated on the moment. "Just wait. It gets better." He nudged Cutter into a walk. The horse's motion rocked them gently against each other.

Her fingers bit into his shoulders. A hard shudder ran through her. "A wicked, wicked man." Her voice was rough and smoky as she leaned forward and delivered a love bite to the base of his neck.

The stinging sensation shot straight to his groin. He pulled her hips forward, rocking into her.

She shivered in his arms. "Too many clothes." She leaned back just enough to get her hands between them. With shaky fingers, she went to work at his silver buckle.

"Good idea." He slid his hands under the hem of her skirt and worked his way slowly up to her thighs, exploring, memorizing every inch of firm muscle and silken skin along the way.

As he pushed her skirt over her hips, a tiny triangle of red silk lace came into view. He groaned softly. "You're killing me here."

She smiled, a woman's smile, one filled with confidence and desire and something else he refused to put a name to. "I thought you might like them."

"Very much. But they gotta go." He hated to ruin the sexy garment, but he didn't see any other way to get it off her beyond tearing one of the tiny bands of elastic slashing across her delectable hips. And the thought of some other cowboy enjoying them at a future date…

With one quick pull, he broke the elastic and slid the other half down her leg, out of his way.

She chuckled softly. "I don't know if I should be offended by that move…or flattered. Although, considering the evidence before me—" she ran her fingers over the bulge of his arousal "—I'm thinking flattered."

"Definitely flattered," he said through gritted teeth. "Do you need some help there?"

"Nope, I'm doing just fine." Her teeth flashed in a sexy, teasing smile as she carefully slid his zipper down.

He sprang free.

She inhaled softly. "Forget flattered, let's move straight to purely impressed."

Fire raced through him. He'd never wanted anything as much as he wanted her, right here, right now. "I'd like to drag this on for hours, but I can't wait any longer." He lowered his head, crushing her lips beneath his. Sliding his hands under her thighs, he lifted her, adjusting her position until the head of his arousal nudged at her soft folds.

She pulled her lips from his just long enough to whisper, "I don't want to wait, either."

A silent prayer of thanks whispered through his head. Slowly, deliberately, he lowered her. Her wet heat wrapped around him like a tight fist. He gritted his teeth, holding on to his control by the barest of threads.

For several steps they clung to each other, letting the gait of the horse tantalize them, tease them.

She ran her hands over his chest, looking up at him, her eyelids at half-mast. "Do you see how good this is? Do you realize how good it could be?"

His heart squeezed again. He couldn't give her what she wanted, but he could give her something to remember. "Shh. Just feel. I'm going to push Cutter into a slow, easy lope." He cued the horse with his legs.

Cutter's haunches dipped down, rocking them backwards as he prepared to change his gait. Then his whithers rose, pushing Tate up, burying him deeper in Crissy's warmth as he rocked forward.

"Ohh." She breathed the exclamation, her fingers closing around his arms, keeping herself balanced as he kept their hips locked together. Another moan whispered from her lips and she rocked back a bit, adjusting her position, taking him deeper.

His gait slow and easy, Cutter rocked them toward ecstasy.

Tate strained a deep, stabilizing breath through his teeth as he struggled to hold on to his control and stared down at the woman in his arms. The woman wrapped around the most intimate part of him. The moonlight glinted off her hair, her breasts, her wet, swollen lips.

So beautiful.

And so damned dear.

She looked into his eyes, letting him see her desire, letting him see how much she wanted him. She hid nothing from him, held nothing back as she took him into her body. Her heart was in her eyes. And she was offering it to him.

The fire blazing through him turned into an inferno. What little control he had slipped away. He wanted all of her. Her body, her heart and her sweet cries of ecstasy echoing in his ears. He nudged Cutter into a faster pace.

Her fingers tightened as the horse's motion pushed him deeper, sharpening her pleasure. His pleasure. Her inner muscles tightened around him, caressing, demanding. But he held on. Waiting. Waiting.

A soft groan slipped from her lips. She snapped tight as a bow, a low, keening wail bursting from her lips as she came apart in his arms.

He followed her with a hard shout of his own, the world exploding around him.

With a single command, he brought Cutter back to a walk and gathered Crissy close, holding her tight. Holding on to her like a dying man holding on to his last, precious breath. Had he thought he could steal this one night, these few moments and then go back to pretending there was nothing between them? That she was no more than his boss?

Fool.

Chapter Fourteen

Last night had been the most incredible night of Tate's life. And it was destined to remain that way. He stepped outside onto his small wooden porch, carrying his duffel. It was early. Not much after five in the morning. But the ranch was already starting the new day.

The sun was half up the horizon. Hank was throwing hay and grain to the horses and cattle in the home corrals. Cowboys were wandering out of the bunkhouse, heading to their trucks and driving to the outer pastures.

After years of living here, he was intimately familiar with the routine. He drew in a breath of the hot, dry air, savoring the combined scent of mesquite and Texas dust, cedar and livestock. It was a sweet fragrance. A fragrance that was uniquely the Big T's. Breathing deeply of it, he shifted his gaze to the big house.

He'd dropped Crissy at her front door a bit after one
last night. The four hours since had been the longest
of his life.

He couldn't get her out of his mind. She was everything he'd ever dreamed of. Everything he'd ever
wanted. Sexy. Caring. Giving. And so damned tough.
She might well have what it took to face a thousand
Caldwells and spit in their eyes. The only problem
was…she shouldn't have to.

Across the way, a light went on in the big house.
Through the big picture windows, he could see her
making her way down the stairs, her soft, stonewashed
jeans hugging her feminine curves, her tank top ac-
centuating her tiny waist and the tantalizing shape of
her breasts.

His fingers tingled. His body readied. His heart
ached. If he needed proof the decision he'd agonized
over all night was the right one, the need pounding
through him right now was it. He drew a deep fortifying breath, took one more look at his surroundings and
forced his feet to move.

He tossed his duffel into his truck and strode across
the road to the big house, his movements heavy and
stiff, as if his legs didn't belong to him. As if they
didn't want to go where he was pushing them.

He'd felt this way once before. When he'd walked
into the state pen all those years ago. He'd thought
walking through those big iron doors had been the
longest, hardest walk of his life.

He'd been wrong.

* * *

Crissy walked into the kitchen in the quiet house. The other girls were still asleep, thank God. She wasn't up to facing them this morning, any more than she had been at 3:00 a.m. when they'd finally wandered home. She'd stayed hidden in her room to avoid them then, but she was glad such measures weren't necessary this morning.

She needed coffee. It had been a long, anxious night. She wanted to believe making love to McCade last night had been a breakthrough. That she'd convinced him there was something between them worth fighting for. But she didn't think she had.

There'd been something about his lovemaking last night. A desperation in the way he'd watched her and touched her and loved her that made her think it was a onetime deal for him. A thought that had been reinforced when he'd dropped her at the door instead of coming in with her or bringing her to his house.

Measuring coffee into the filter, she tried to calm the nagging sense of dread. She might be misreading the whole thing. He might have dropped her at her door because he didn't think the best way to announce their relationship was to have the entire ranch population find them in bed together. He might think it was better if the hands saw them dating first.

Except he hadn't said anything about future dates. About future anything.

She closed the coffee basket, flicked the machine on and took a deep steadying breath. If he was trying to close her out, she wasn't going to let him. Not after what they'd shared last night. It had been too good. *He* was too good to let get away, dang it. And she was going to let him know it. Just as soon as she bolstered her nerve with a little caffeine.

A knock sounded on her front door.

She startled. Who on earth was knocking on her door at five o'clock in the morning? She hurried to the door and pulled it open.

McCade stood on her porch, hat in hand.

His expression was an unreadable mask, but she didn't think she'd ever seen such desolation in a person's eyes. Her stomach plummeted, and a cold sweat broke out on her palms. "Is there a problem on the ranch?" Please, let there be something wrong with the ranch.

He shook his head. "As far as I know everything's running smoothly."

Oh, God. She swallowed hard, the fear she'd been fighting all night swamping her. "Then why are you here?" It obviously wasn't to pick up where they'd left off last night or he wouldn't be crushing his hat in his hands. He'd be reaching for her.

He looked away, a muscle along his jaw working.

Her stomach crashed to her toes.

Finally, he looked back, meeting her gaze. "I came by to let you know I'm leaving. I know this is short notice, but with roundup behind us, there isn't anything crucial going on. I've left a list of men on my table I think are best qualified to be foreman. Have

Braxton help you make a decision. He won't steer you wrong."

She could barely make sense of the words. "You're leaving?"

He nodded. "Tell Braxton I'll get in touch with him for my last paycheck once I'm resettled."

She shook her head, panic racing through her. "Oh, no. I am not going to just let you walk away. Not after last night."

"After last night, it's the only thing I can do."

"What the heck does *that* mean?"

His lips thinned into a hard, uncompromising line. "You know what it means."

"No, I don't. And you're not leaving until I do."

"We've already had this conversation. Nothing's changed."

"Have you lost your mind? *Everything's* changed."

He shook his head. "All last night did was prove I can't keep my hands off you. It didn't change who I am. *What* I am."

"Oh, for—we're back to the stupid ex-con thing."

"There's nothing stupid about it. I won't risk your reputation by having your name linked to mine in anything other than a working relationship. And after last night, it's pretty clear to me I'm not capable of keeping my hands to myself where you're concerned."

"I don't consider having to face a few bigots a risk worth noticing. And the fact that you can't keep your hands to yourself around me isn't a bad thing. It means you're as attracted to me as I am to you. And in my book, that's a good thing. A very good thing."

"If I was any other man in the world, it might be a good thing. But I'm not any other man. I'm a man who tried to kill another man."

She tossed a hand in frustration. "*Thirteen years ago.*"

He shook his head. "Time doesn't negate some things. Having a prison record is one of them. I'm leaving, Crissy. End of story." He turned on his heel and strode toward his truck.

She grabbed hold of him and pulled him back. "You're being ridiculous. I don't care what other people think."

"You might not. But I do. And your father would have cared, too."

"What does my father have to do with anything?"

"A lot. Before he died, he made me promise I'd make sure you had everything that was good and wonderful and bright in this world. And, by God, I'm going to keep that promise." He pulled out of her grasp and strode away.

She stared after him, her heart shredding into a million pieces. She wanted to run to him, make him listen to her. But it wouldn't do her any good. She had only to look at the stiff line of his back to know he'd made up his mind.

He was leaving.

She watched him walk to his truck, crawl in and drive away, tears pouring down her cheeks. Would she never get this man thing right?

Chapter Fifteen

Crissy sat listlessly on the cowhide sofa in the living room, staring out at the Big T. It was almost noon. The sun was approaching its zenith, its heat busily baking the Texas soil. The cowboys were flocking to the bunk-house, coming in from the barns and the closer ranges for lunch. She shifted her gaze from the daily hustle and bustle and stared at the little house across the road.

The house that had been Tate's.

Pain clawed at her heart and the numbing sensation she'd been battling since he'd left two weeks ago got a little deeper.

Josie came into the room, pouting as she spied Crissy on the sofa. "You're not sitting around brooding again, are you?"

Pulling herself from her stupor, Crissy mustered

what energy she could and shoved it into an expression that hopefully made her look cheery. "No. I'm just sitting here…"

"Brooding," Josie filled in with a knowing look.

What energy Crissy'd managed to gather leaked out of her like air from a balloon. "Yeah."

Josie dropped down onto the sofa beside her. "This is pitiful. You realize that, don't you? You're acting like an idiot. Quit lying around mooning over this guy. Go out and learn how to chase cows or something."

"Cattle. Learn how to chase cattle. And there's no point in that."

"Why not?"

"Because I'm not going to stay." There, she'd said it. She ought to be glad the only person she had to say it to was Josie. Mattie and Nell had headed back to their own homes last week.

Josie's brows crumpled in confusion. "You're not staying? Are you going to sell the place then?"

She shook her head. "I still want to use it as a base for the charity. But I'll get someone else to run it. Braxton, maybe. As the financial man, he knows better than anyone what it will take to keep the place going. Once I'm gone, he can hire a foreman to keep the day-to-day operations running smoothly." She hadn't been able to hire anyone to take Tate's place. It just seemed…wrong, somehow.

"But if you leave, where will you go?" Concern filled Josie's voice.

"Back to my place in Denver."

"Oh, no, you are not going back to that godforsaken hole-in-the-wall where your only company will be the cockroaches living under your sink." She pushed up from the sofa and paced away. When she turned back, her eyes crackled with stubborn determination. "This is ridiculous. You can't walk away from the most decent home you've ever known just because McCade did. The man is gone. Snap out of it and get on with your life."

Fresh pain slashed through her. "You don't have to tell me he's gone, Josie. I'm well aware of that fact."

"Then stop acting like a thirteen-year-old with a broken heart and get back into the game. Think about some of the fund-raisers we talked about using the ranch for. The cowboy auction. The rodeo."

Crissy thrust up from the sofa. "I don't want to think about those things. They both require being here. And I don't want to be here anymore, period. It's too painful. Everywhere I look, I see him. I go out to play with Little Moe and I see Tate helping me deliver him. I look at the Santa Gertrudis in the corrals and I picture him on the range the day he took me out to roundup. Yesterday I took a ride out to Pillar Creek and—" Her voice broke and tears flooded her eyes. She spun away, swiping at the tears. She wasn't going to break down in front of Josie, dang it.

"Oh, my God." Josie whispered, dropping back onto the sofa. "You love him."

Crissy spun back, shaking her head. "Don't be ridiculous. It's just…"

"Just what?" Josie demanded.

Crissy's heart raced. She'd already lost too many people she loved. Her mother, way too early for a child to be saying goodbye to a parent. Her father, before she'd even known him. She didn't want to add the man she loved to that list.

She strode over to the window, panic pushing at her. She didn't love him. She *didn't*. She stared out at the corrals looking for a distraction, anything to keep her from thinking about the words pounding through her head, the emotions squeezing the air from her. But the yard was quiet, everyone had gone into the bunkhouse to eat.

She tried to concentrate on the horses standing nose to tail and gently scratching each other's rumps in the nearest corral. But her gaze slid sideways until she was staring, once again, at Tate's house. She dropped her head against the cool pane of glass with a defeated groan. She could deny the words all she wanted, but there was no denying the pain in her heart.

She loved him.

God help her, she loved him. She turned back to Josie, her shoulders slumping as she leaned against the glass. "Now what?"

Her expression sympathetic, Josie came over and put her arms around her. She held her quietly for a minute, then pulled back just far enough to look into her eyes. "If you love this guy, you can't give up this easy. You can't give up on this ranch and you can't give up on him. You've got to go after him. Fight for him."

She shook her head. "He's not going to give in, Josie. He's too damned stubborn. Too damned…honorable."

Josie waved away her comments. "Honor, schmonor. You're not buying that nonsense about him tainting you, are you?"

"I've never bought it and you know it. But that doesn't mean he doesn't buy it. And in case you haven't heard, it takes two to tango."

"I'm not asking you about the tango. I'm asking you if you believe he's not worthy of you."

"Oh, for pity's sake. He is the most decent man I've ever met. Any woman would be lucky to have him in her life."

"Well, then, pardon my bluntness, but you need to quit sitting here like some sorry quitter. You need to pack your bags and go out and get him."

Quitter.

The word caught in her mind, jogging another memory.

I can't believe Warner's daughter is this much of a quitter.

Tate's words echoed in her head, followed by others, equally pointed.

From what you said, leaving at the first sign of trouble and never looking back was a habit of hers. Before you decide to walk away from the Big T, make sure this isn't one of your mother's traits you're glomming on to.

She'd made up her mind that night she wouldn't

give up easily again. But she had. Not on the ranch, but on something far, far more important.

Shame on her.

She straightened her shoulders. "You're right, I wimped out. And…that's enough of that. Come on, you can help me—oh, geez, major problem."

"What's that?" Josie asked.

"I don't know where Tate is. Even if I wanted to toss a rope around him and tie him down until he listened, I don't know where to find him. He called Braxton right after he left, told him he'd let him know when he'd be staying some place long enough to have his check sent, but so far he hasn't made that call."

"Okay, that's going to be a tricky roadblock. But we can get around it."

"*How?*" Desperation froze her brain.

"I don't know, but we'll think of something. Maybe you could put an ad in the paper, threatening to burn the place down if he doesn't get his cute little cowboy behind back here."

Crissy shot her a disparaging look. "What paper would that be? For all we know, he's in Alaska somewhere. Or Timbuktu."

"I see your point."

"Wait a minute." Hope surged through her as her idea began to take shape. "The Angels always get national press—and air time."

Josie nodded. "We do, but we can't go on TV and threaten to burn the ranch down."

Crissy laughed, feeling more alive than she had in

days. "No, we can't. But Tate's not wild about the Angel stunts. I think a risky one might bring him running."

Catching on, Josie smiled. "Got one in mind?"

An article she'd read in a travel magazine a few months back popped into Crissy's head. She smiled wickedly. "As a matter of fact, I do. Let's go call the other girls."

Tate strode into his hotel room in Oklahoma with the bag of burgers and fries he'd picked up across the street. The last three weeks had been the longest of his life. Longer than the five years he'd spent behind bars. He missed the Big T.

He missed Crissy.

Swearing softly, he set his dinner on the small table by the bed and toed his boots off. "Get over it, fool. You made the right decision." The *only* decision he could make if he was going to keep his promise to Crissy's father.

Which didn't make him stop missing her. Didn't make him stop wanting her.

He propped the bed pillows against the headboard, sat, kicked his stockinged feet out in front of him and grabbed the white paper bag, wishing to hell it was a bottle of Cuervo Gold instead. The last thing he felt like doing was eating. But nursing a bottle of tequila until he passed out…that had definite appeal.

Too much appeal for a man who didn't have anything in his life to stay sober for. So he'd forgone the bottle for the bag of food. Pulling a burger out, he stared at the ugly painting tacked on the wall above the TV. God, he was sick of motel rooms. He needed to get back to work. If he had something to occupy his time, his hands, maybe he'd stop thinking about Crissy.

Stop thinking about how beautiful she was. Stop thinking about the way her breasts had filled his hands. Or the way she'd looked at him the night they'd made love. He closed his eyes, trying to ignore his body's response.

He definitely needed to get back to work. The problem was, the only places hiring in this neck of the woods were small spreads. Spreads he could keep running with his eyes closed. He needed a big, demanding ranch, one that would challenge him mentally and physically if he was going to stay sane. And there didn't seem to be one here in Oklahoma.

Maybe he'd try Colorado. Or Wyoming. He'd heard there were big ranches in Wyoming. And it was farther from Texas. Maybe a little more distance between him and Crissy would help him to forget her, too. Yeah. Wyoming sounded good. Decision made, he grabbed the remote and flicked on the TV. He'd catch the end of the news while he finished his dinner and then he'd head down the road.

The national news reporter, his gray hair perfectly styled, stared out at the audience with a smile on his lips.

The Alpine Angels are at it again. They've scheduled a fund-raiser for a young girl with leukemia.

Ashley Martin's family lives outside of Taos, New Mexico, and is in need of funds to help pay for their daughter's chemotherapy. The Angels are stepping outside their usual alpine venue for this stunt and heading for the deep blue. They're having a shark rodeo off the coast of the Bahamas, feeding and riding the sharks in those crystalline waters to raise money. They've got the Suny and Milo corporations on the hook for a thousand dollars for each fish the world's most deadly eating machines take off the Angels' spears. Five thousand for each fish they take out of the Angels' hands. And ten thousand dollars for each "ride" the Angels take holding on to the sharks' dorsal fins. It promises to be quite an event. For those interested in adding to the pot, an e-mail address will be flashed at the end of the program.

Tate stared at the TV, his blood running cold, the burger in his hand all but forgotten as the commentator moved on to the next story.

Sharks.

They were going to feed sharks? From their hands? And then they were going to blithely grab hold of their dorsal fins for a little ride?

Over his dead body.

Tossing his dinner aside, he stood and snatched the phone from its place on the bedside table. He punched the ranch's number in, stabbing each button with the anger building inside him as he paced away from the bed—until the short hotel cord brought him to an abrupt halt. Dammit.

The phone rang on the other end.

Once.

Twice.

"Big T." Brax's voice.

"What the hell do you think you're doing, letting those girls head down to the Bahamas to feed sharks, for crying out loud?"

"Ah, you must have just caught the news. CBS did a good job, don't you think? The girls should make some good bucks with this stunt."

"Good—have you lost your damn mind? They'll probably get eaten alive."

"Crissy says not, though I imagine they could." Braxton's voice was amazingly calm considering the words coming out of his mouth.

"Then stop them, dammit."

"I'm not their mommy. And neither are you. In fact, you don't have any say at all over what they do. More to the point, what *Crissy* does. You're out of her life, remember?"

He stilled. There was something far too smug in Brax's tone. "Is this a setup? Is Crissy just trying to lure me back within her grasp?"

"She hasn't said so. She's playing it straight, hasn't mentioned she has any other motivation for the fundraiser beyond Ashley's need."

"But—" Tate pushed.

"But there's a calculating gleam in her eye that's pretty hard to miss." There wasn't an ounce of empathy in Brax's voice.

"And knowing that, you didn't stop her."

"Like I said, not my job."

Anger raced through him. What the hell was Brax thinking? He knew the man hadn't been happy at Tate's leaving. Brax had made himself clear on that subject when Tate had called right after he'd left. But when all was said and done, he thought his friend had at least understood that he didn't belong in Crissy's life, that his leaving was the only option available. Apparently not. "Anything happens to any of those girls, Crissy in particular, I'm coming after you."

"You know where to find me."

"Count on it. In the meantime, where and when is this little shindig taking place?" His gut clenched as he realized he'd have to chase after her. Have to put an end to this nonsense himself.

"Day after tomorrow off the shores of Great Abaco in the Bahamas. Their final meeting with the press before they head out on the boat is at 7:00 a.m. You'd best get a move on if you want to get there before Crissy feeds her arm to a shark. Have fun. Say hi to the girls and—"

Tate slammed the phone down and paced away, struggling for a calming breath, glad he was as far from Braxton as he was.

Say hi to the girls?

Sure.
Right after he wrung their necks.
Crissy's first.

Chapter Sixteen

Tate stood in the small speedboat, his legs spread, his knees loose and both hands holding on to the windshield as they sped over the choppy waves of the Caribbean Sea. Cowboy boots might be just the trick for ranch work, but they sucked on a boat pounding the waves. Not that he gave a damn. At the moment the only thing of importance was getting to the *Sea Breeze*, the boat the Angels were using as their platform for the shark-feeding expedition.

He'd missed the press conference in the hotel. His plane hadn't been late, thankfully, but the only flight he'd been able to snag on such late notice had put him on Great Abaco fifteen minutes after the press conference had ended. Now he was playing catch-up, hoping to hell he made it to the boat before the girls went overboard.

His heart pounding, his palms cold and sweaty, he glanced over at the man whose services and boat he'd hired. The islander's attention was focused on the *Sea Breeze.* The throttle was full-bore. Little point in pushing the boat driver to go faster. He couldn't. He was eking out every bit of speed his small boat had.

As they got closer to the *Sea Breeze,* Tate noticed she was fairly big, around eighty feet. A tall cabin with deck space on top took up most of the center portion of the boat. There was a small deck area aft, with a narrow walkway that ran along the side to a larger deck area at the prow.

Almost everyone was at the prow. He imagined they were gathered around the big TV screen that was always present at the Angel events. No doubt little Ashley and her family would be there, along with several news reporters, representatives from the corporations and other people who'd pledged smaller money donations.

He desperately searched for the girls. Four bright pink wet suits with blond heads topping them caught his eye. The girls were still on board.

Thank God.

His boat powered down as they approached. As his driver got them snuggled up next to the *Sea Breeze,* Tate quickly took in the party going on up front.

A big shark swam by on the large screen, its open jaw displaying its sharp, deadly teeth. Tate's gut jerked into a tight knot and he pulled his gaze from the deadly predator. He spotted Ashley. She was sitting front and center in a lounge chair. She looked to be about six. Her long, dark hair trailed over her shoulder accenting her unnaturally pale complexion.

Angelic.

That was the word that came to mind as he stared at the little girl. He was glad Crissy and the other Angels were helping her. *But,* not in the manner they'd chosen. They had other ways to make money now. Safer ways.

With the small boat bobbing beneath the *Sea Breeze*'s ladder, Tate grabbed hold of the metal rungs and climbed onto the big boat's gently rocking deck. He started up the narrow walkway that led to the prow, looking for Crissy. He picked her out of the crowd fairly quickly. She was talking to a gray-haired man in a business suit, an animated smile on her lips.

She spotted Tate making his way to her. Triumph chased across her face as she realized her little ploy to get him here had worked. She quickly passed the businessman off to Josie, whispered something in her friend's ear and headed his way.

He drank in the sight of her. The way her hair spilled in golden curls from the ponytail fixed on top of her head. The way the tight, bright pink wet suit hugged her every tantalizing curve. The way her hips kicked in seductive invitation as she made her way to him. She looked good. Damned good.

But he wasn't here to admire her beauty.

He was here to wring her neck. He stopped at the end of the walkway, waited for her to close the distance between them and pinned her with a hard gaze. "What the *hell* do you think you're doing?"

She winced at his words and peeked over her shoulder, obviously worrying if anyone had heard. But no one was paying attention to them. Josie had dragged the businessman in front of the big screen and was addressing the crowd, keeping their attention there. Crissy took his elbow and started pulling him toward the back of the boat.

He followed because the last thing Ashley and her family needed was more strife in their lives. But as soon as he and Crissy reached the back of the boat, he pulled her around to face him. "Answer my question, dammit. What the hell do you think you're doing?"

She batted her lashes innocently. "Isn't that evident? We're holding another Alpine Angels event."

"Don't jerk my chain, Crissy. You won't like the result. This event wasn't designed to save that little girl. It was designed to bring me running."

She squared her shoulders and met his gaze head on. "This is absolutely about making sure Ashley gets the medical treatments she needs. But was the specific event chosen to get your cute little cowboy butt here? You bet."

He narrowed his eyes on her. "And getting me here is worth risking your friends' safety?"

"No, it isn't." she spat. "That's your fault."

"Excuse me?" he asked incredulously.

"Look, I came up with this idea because I knew you'd come running when you heard we were going to feed sharks. But that's all we were going to do originally. *Feed* the sharks. No big deal."

"No big deal?" he asked pointedly. "They're *sharks,* Crissy. Big, deadly, eating machines with monster jaws and row after row of razor-sharp teeth. They're not a bunch of trained poodles."

"And we weren't going to try to make them to jump through hoops. We were just going to throw them a few tasty morsels of fish. *That* was my idea. You and I talked about this, remember? I want to keep my friends around for a long, long time. I want to start making these events safer. And the shark psychologists—"

"Shark *psychologists?* For crying out loud, don't tell me you listened to people who call themselves shark *psychologists.* You think those animals come in and lie on couches?"

She shot him a disparaging look. "Fine. Call them whatever you want. The point is these guys study sharks. They know how the animals think. They assured me feeding them is perfectly safe. In fact, they feed them here all the time. It's no biggie. They even let the tourists do it."

"Stupid, foolish tourists, maybe."

She waved away his words. "Nobody's ever been hurt doing it, so it's obviously safe. It just sounds and looks dangerous, which made it the perfect stunt to get the corporations to pledge their money and—"

"Get me to come running. Yeah, I got that part."

She jutted her chin into the air. "Good. Anyway,

then Mattie got it in her head that we could up the corporate pledges if we rode the beasts." She tossed her hands in exasperation, shaking her head. "A shark rodeo. What the heck was *she* thinking?"

"You expect me to believe you girls don't talk about these decisions?"

"I expect you to be astute enough to realize if I went to all this trouble to get you here, I'm not going to waste my time lying to you. As for the decision bit, yes, we usually decide on the event details together. But since you left, I've been a little…distracted. Mattie thought she was doing me a favor by making the decision herself. By the time she let me in on her plans, she'd already talked to the corporations *and* the press. It was a done deal, nothing I could do about it."

"You could have put a stop to it."

She shook her head. "Not without hurting this fundraiser. We've built our reputation on wild, dangerous stunts. Putting an end to the rodeo part of the event would have made us look like scaredy-cats. No way would the corporations have pledged money for that. And Ashley is counting on that money for the treatment she needs. I'm not going to let her down."

The knot in his gut pulled tighter. Of course they couldn't let her down. He stabbed his fingers through his hair. "Dammit. Everything was fine when I left. What the hell happened?"

"What do you mean everything was fine? *I* wasn't fine." She pointed at her chest with an angry finger.

"You would have been. In time, you would have

been." He couldn't stand the pain he saw in her face. Couldn't stand that he'd put it there. He paced away, curling his hands into tight fists. "Dammit. Promising Warner I'd bring you home was stupid. I'd already screwed up one family. What the hell made me think I could help his?"

"Don't tell me I would have been fine. You don't get to make that call. And what does that mean? You'd already screwed up one family?"

"It doesn't mean anything." He paced away. That was the last road he wanted to go down.

"Oh, no. You can't back out of that statement now. I think it's important." She strode over and pulled him around, her gaze sharp and intense. "Do you blame yourself for your sister's rape?"

Panic nipped at his heels. "Don't be ridiculous. How the hell could I have been responsible for my sister's rape? She was at a school dance. My dad dropped her at the school's doors. She was there with a hundred other kids. She should have been perfectly safe. No one could have known Caldwell would drag her out the back door and rape her in the alley."

She shuddered at the harsh reality of his words, but her gaze didn't waver. "What about what happened after? Her death? Do you blame yourself for that?"

He couldn't breathe. Couldn't think. It was as if a giant hand was squeezing the life out of him.

"Answer me, dammit."

"Yes." The word was out of his mouth before he could stop it. "Yes, I blame myself. If I hadn't gone after that bastard, if I hadn't been so intent on proving how big a man I was, I wouldn't have been in jail the night my sister ran her car off the cliff. I might have been around to take the keys from her. And if I'd done that, maybe my parents wouldn't have had to bury their daughter."

"Oh, God." She closed her eyes momentarily. When she opened them, empathy spiked with determination glistened there. "I'm not going to tell you you're wrong. If you hadn't gone after Caldwell's son, if you'd been at home, maybe you would have saved Leanne that night. But you might not have, either. Teenage girls are sneaky. And innovative. I can't tell you how many times I told my mom I was going over to a friends to study when the local honky-tonk—the one where they looked the other way for minors if you slipped a ten to the guy at the door—was our real destination. And even if you'd saved her that night, it doesn't mean you would have saved her the next time. She's not blameless for what happened to her."

"She was a sixteen-year-old girl who'd been brutally raped."

"Yes, she was. She was young and hurt and, like you, she made some bad choices."

"She's not responsible for those choices, she was hurting too badly. *I,* on the other hand, was simply trying to stoke my ego, prove how big a man I was." And he hated himself for it.

She shook her head. "You're *not* going to sell me that. And if you've been selling it to yourself all these years, you're obviously still trying to hang on to all that male pride. Caldwell's son might not have attacked you, but you were hurting, too. Not physically, but emotionally."

"You can hardly compare my anger to the pain she was going through. If she made mistakes it was hardly her fault, but me—"

"Don't." She pinned him with a steely glare. "Don't you dare belittle the emotions you were feeling then. Were you angry someone had hurt your sister? I'm sure you were. Livid. But don't pretend it was the only emotion you felt. Or even the strongest one. You forget, I know what it's like to see someone you love hurting—physically, mentally. I stood over my mother's bed and watched a nightmarish disease ravage her. I saw her pain every minute of every day. And it hurt like hell. Don't try telling me your sister's pain didn't hurt you."

"Even if it did, it was no excuse for going after Caldwell."

"No, it wasn't. But it would certainly have been one heck of an impetus. God knows, there were days if I'd thought killing someone would make my mom feel better, I might have pounded someone to a bloody pulp myself."

"No, you wouldn't have."

"Don't count on it, cowboy. There were some black days back then."

One look at the shadows in her eyes and he knew there had been. But he couldn't let that sway him.

"You're talking theories. I'm talking reality. You didn't go after anyone. I did. And I not only sealed my sister's fate by doing that, I destroyed my parents' lives as well. Do you have any idea what it was like for them to have one child dead and the other locked up as an attempted murderer?" He shook his head, pain washing through him. "All their hopes, all their dreams flushed down the toilet. And I did it. I won't risk ruining another family."

Her eyes went wide. "Oh, my God. That's why you left. The real reason you left. Not because you were afraid I couldn't handle a few bigots. But because—"

"It's not *the* reason." He stalked away, panic stampeding after him. "It's just another reason. I can give you a dozen more if you've got an hour or so and a sofa. I could lie down for you and you could psychoanalyze me all day long if you like."

"If I get you prone, cowboy, psychoanalyzing you will be the last thing on my mind." Her voice was low, husky.

Desire slammed through him, hot and hard and powerful. He had to put an end to this conversation before it completely ambushed him. And then find a way to stop her and the others from riding those sharks.

"Crissy, it's time to go." The female voice broke into their argument.

Startled, they both turned to find Mattie peeking around the corner.

The tall statuesque blonde tipped her head toward the front of the boat. "It's time."

Crissy gave her head a quick nod. "I'll be right there. You guys head on down." She turned back to him. "I don't have time to pussyfoot around here, so I'll get right to the point. You made a mistake once. A big one. One that affected people's lives. But you've paid for that mistake. More importantly, you've learned from it. Does that mean you'll never make another one? Probably not. Fallibility is part of the human condition. But—"

"I don't need a lecture on mistakes. I—"

"You're going to get one, anyway. You told me once you thought of all the mistakes my folks made, my mother made the biggest one when she walked away without giving herself and my dad the chance to make things right. How is what you're doing any different?"

"Oh, for crying out—it's completely different."

She shook her head. "No, actually, it's not. You might be running for different reasons. But you're still running, cowboy. The question you have to ask yourself is do you want to behave like my mother? Or my father? Dad made as big a mistake as Mom did twenty-two years ago. The difference was, he dug in and did what he could to rectify the situation. And he didn't do it just for himself and his family; he did it for others, too. He did it for the cowboys that work on the ranch. He did it for you. He gave you a second chance, Tate. Don't throw that back in his face."

She turned from him and started back toward the aisle that led to the front of the boat, but she turned on her heel and came back to him. "I love you, Tate McCade."

The words hit him like a sucker punch.

She chuckled softly and shook her head. "I'm not going to take it back, so live with it. I love you. And I'm not willing to let the best thing that's ever wandered into my life wander out. So do us both a favor. Make the right decision here. Screw up some courage and give us a chance." She raised on her toes and kissed him, hard and deep. Then she turned on her heel and strode away.

He watched her go, his world spinning around him. *She loved him?*

He swallowed hard, her words about her mother and father echoing in his head. Was she right? Was he running?

He stared at her as she donned her diving gear and stepped off the side of the boat. Her image appeared on the giant screen as she slowly sank toward the bottom of the sea. Big, sleek, torpedo-shaped animals appeared in the background.

Sharks.

Damn.

She settled on the bottom of the sea and took a spear from a diver already kneeling there, a big fish skewered on the end. A shark darted her way, his sleek body racing through the water, his deadly jaws gaping.

Why did he get the feeling if he didn't want to spend the rest of his life watching Crissy go from one hair-raising stunt after the next, he'd better come to terms with his past.

* * *

Her heart pounding a frantic tattoo, Crissy held on to the shark's dorsal fin as it thrashed through the water, trying to dislodge her.

One thousand one.

One thousand two.

Eight seconds. Like the bull riders in the rodeo, she had to stay with the shark for eight seconds. She gritted her teeth and held on for dear life as the sharp-edged, sandpapery hide bit into her skin.

One thousand four.

One thousand five.

The shark jerked toward her, its jaws opened wide, its sharp, jagged teeth a clear warning as the shark tried to make her let go. Oh, God. She closed her eyes and held on tighter. As long as she was snuggled up to his side he couldn't reach her.

One thousand seven.

One thousand eight.

She let go as the shark jerked in the other direction—away from her—and held her breath to see if the angry fish would turn back toward her to bite her in half or swim away.

It darted into the murky depths.

Thank God.

She sucked in a deep breath of compressed air and looked for the other girls, praying they were okay. Praying she wouldn't find body parts and a trail of blood floating through the water. She found them together, elbows linked not far away. They all waved heartily. Relief poured through her. They were okay.

It had been a successful event. They'd made money on all but one of the fish the dive masters had brought down for them to feed. And they'd all ridden their sharks. Ashley's parents wouldn't have to worry about what they could and couldn't afford for their daughter. Ashley would get every medical treatment she needed.

Now all they had to do was get out of the sea without one of the sharks wandering back for a last tasty bite. Crissy pointed toward the surface with her thumb, signaling it was time to head up. But first, the four of them turned to the underwater cameramen, took their regulators out of their mouths, smiled widely and waved to the people on the boat. Then they were all heading up.

As Crissy swam toward the surface, keeping a sharp eye on the few sharks that still swam around looking for another handout, her thoughts shifted to Tate. Would he still be there when she got back on board? Or would he be gone? Her stomach tied in a thousand knots.

Let him be there.

Please, let him be there.

She hit the surface, handed her vest with the heavy air tank and her fins off to a helper and scampered up the ladder to the *Sea Breeze*'s deck, hoping the first face she'd see would be his. But he wasn't in the crowd that greeted her.

Her heart sank and she searched deeper into the layers of people crowding around her, but he was nowhere to be seen. Tears stung her eyes. She did her best to blink them back, glad for the camouflaging effect of the sea's wetness.

"Crissy. Crissy." The small voice belonged to Ashley.

The crowd in front of Crissy parted and the wraith-like child made her way through.

Crissy forced her lips into a big smile. "Hey, girl, what'd you think?"

Ashley giggled. "I think I'm never going to get into that sea. Those sharks would swallow me whole."

Crissy laughed with her. "I think you're right. We'll have to think of something else fun for you to do when you get through with all your treatments. How about… I know, a trip to Disney World?"

"Yea!" Ashley jumped up and down. "Will Mickey be there?"

"I bet he will be. You can say hi for me."

Ashley's parents had moved in behind her. Worried frowns furrowed their brows.

Crissy moved quickly to reassure them. "The trip is compliments of the Alpine Angels, of course. Your only job is to make sure she gets healthy so she can enjoy the trip."

Linda, Ashley's mom, smiled, tears springing to her eyes. "We can do that. And we wanted to thank you girls. You've truly been angels to us. If you hadn't done this…" She swiped at her tears, doing her best to hang on to her composure.

"No thanks necessary. You just take care of this little girl." Crissy gave Linda's arm a reassuring squeeze and stepped away, giving the parents time to compose themselves.

That's when she saw him.

He was standing in the alcove that led down below, his cowboy boots looking a bit out of place on the boat, his cowboy hat held tightly in his hands, his intense gaze tracking her every move.

He'd stayed.

A little bubble of hope pushed at her throat. Did his presence mean he'd decided to give them a chance? Or just that he'd stayed to say goodbye? Hope and fear pounding through her, she made her way across the deck. She wanted to throw herself into his arms, but she stopped a few feet away, giving him a little breathing room. "You're still here."

The corners of his lips quirked. "So it appears."

"Does that mean…" She plowed her fingers through her hair. She was afraid to ask the question. But she was more afraid not to. "Does that mean you're going to give us a chance?"

He looked away, the tiny smile disappearing as he gazed out at the vast expanse of water. "It means I think you're right about why I left. It scares me to death to think of starting a relationship, a family, and then making a big mistake down the road that would tear it apart."

Was that an I'm-leaving or I'm-staying comment? Afraid to tip the scale the wrong way, she stuck to a true, but unavoidable, observation. "Life is scary sometimes."

He laughed humorlessly. "If the last twenty minutes is any indication, it can be damned terrifying."

Since there wasn't one single bone in her body that disagreed with that, she kept her mouth closed.

He looked at her, his brown-eyed gaze piercing. "I'm never going through that again, Crissy. Ever. Which means running is no longer an option. You obviously need someone around to rein you in."

She stilled. That kind of sounded like an I'm-staying. "Are you by any chance thinking you might do the reining in?"

"I'm sure as hell not going to let any other cowboy do it."

That was definitely an I'm-staying. The bubble of hope burst into joy. But she held herself in check. He'd made her work too hard getting him here for her to let him off too easy. She raised a brow. "Is that right?"

"Absolutely right." He pulled her to him and lowered his lips to hers.

The kiss was hot and deep and left no doubt in her mind that he was staking his claim.

Her knees went weak. Her every nerve ending short-circuited.

Finally, he pulled his lips from hers. "I love you."

She held on to him, gasping for air, the words ringing like sweet chimes in her ears. "In that case, I can live with the macho reining-in thing."

He chuckled, low and sexy. "Glad to hear it. How do you feel about getting married?"

What? She leaned back in his arms to get a good look at his face.

He looked down at her, his expression dead serious.

"Man," she said. "When you screw up your courage, you don't stop halfway, do you?"

"In case you haven't noticed, I'm not a man of half measures. If I'm going to do something, I don't play at it. I do it." He tucked a wet curl behind her ear. "And your father wouldn't like his daughter playing house. If you were sleeping with a man, he'd want you married. And I fully intend to be sleeping with you."

Desire shot through her. Hot and wild. She pulled his lips back to hers and did a little claiming of her own.

Several minutes later, he pulled his lips from hers again, his gaze delving into hers. "Is that a yes?"

She smiled up at him, tears of joy filling her eyes. "It's a yes, cowboy. Yes, yes, yes."

Epilogue

The guests, all dressed in their Sunday best, chatted and joked and laughed as they milled about her father's giant living room, sipping sparkling champagne and munching on tasty hors d'oeuvres. Promise and expectation filled the cavernous room, humming like clear crystalline bells, making the smiles brighter, the laughter sweeter.

Crissy's wedding dress rustled softly as she grabbed another glass of champagne off a passing tray. Now where was her husband? Ah, there he was, across the room talking to Braxton. She sipped at the sparkling wine, savoring the sight of him. He looked gorgeous in his western-cut tails and burgundy vest.

"Stop drooling over the man, it's embarrassing." Mattie stepped next to her, sipping from her own glass of amber bubbles.

Crissy just kept staring. "I can't help it. Just look at him. He's—"

"Gorgeous," Josie said, joining them with Nell in tow. "We know. You tell us a hundred times a day."

"Well, he is. He's also sweet and sexy and—"

"Stop it already," Mattie wailed. "You're just trying to make us jealous."

Crissy laughed. "Hey, Texas is a big state. If you want a cowboy, go out and find one."

"Now you're trying to get rid of us," Josie teased.

But Crissy knew it wasn't all in jest. She knew Josie, who considered the Alpine Angels the only family she'd ever had, was worried about losing that family. Crissy shook her head, locking her gaze on Josie's. "I'm not trying to get rid of you and you know it. You guys are always welcome here. In fact, if you don't spend a fair amount of time here, this house is going to get lonely."

"You're still planning on moving into Tate's house, huh?" Nell asked.

Crissy nodded. "This one's too big for me. Tate's house is a lot more cozy. So you guys will have to come often, fill this one up."

As if sensing the three women staring their way, Tate and Braxton looked over and then headed their way.

As they joined the girls, Braxton looked to Crissy. "So how does it feel to be the official owner of the Big T?"

She and Tate had planned their wedding to coincide with the signing over of the ranch. It had seemed like a long time to wait when they'd come back from Great Abaco. But she'd liked the idea of bringing her life together in one fell swoop. She'd signed both her wedding license and the deed to the ranch with everyone watching not half an hour ago. "Good. It feels good. I can't wait to have the first Alpine Angels event here."

Tate groaned. "Never a moment of peace."

Crissy laughed. "Hey, you were the big push behind more sedate events. A rodeo here ought to make you happy."

"That's what you decided on, the rodeo?" Braxton asked.

Mattie nodded. "We thought the cowboy auction might be too big a step down in action for our first Big T event. A rodeo ought to be perfect."

Crissy looked to Tate. "You said Tommy Ray would be the man to talk to about that, right?"

Tate nodded. "He's the man with the buckles. He'll be able to tell you everything you need to know."

"If you introduce me today, I could start planning," Mattie said.

Tate shook his head. "Weddings aren't Tommy Ray's thing. You'll have to catch him another time."

"Hey, Tate." One of the cowboy's stepped up to their little group. "There's a man outside with a big truck. Says he's supposed to see the bride and groom."

Tate smiled. "That would be my delivery. Thanks, Jimmy."

"Your delivery?" Crissy asked. "What are you having delivered on our wedding day?"

"Something for you. Come see." Tate took her glass and set both his and hers on a passing tray, tucked her arm inside his elbow and led her away. As they made their way toward the door he looked down at her. "Are you having fun?"

"I am. Everything is beautiful. But I'm a little worried about Josie. She's looking a little lost."

He patted her hand. "Give her time. Once she realizes she's welcome here, that you don't intend to cut her out of your life, she'll be fine."

"You're probably right. But still…I'm thinking maybe I should get her a family of her own. We—"

"For crying out loud, don't start matchmaking. You'll have cowboys running for their lives, and we've got fall roundup coming up."

She laughed. "Are you kidding. They find out Josie's the prize, cowboys will be flocking to this ranch like lemmings to the sea."

His lips twisted ruefully. "You have a point. But let's not worry about Josie now, okay?"

She smiled up at him. "You're right. Today is our day." She followed him out onto the porch.

A big work truck with wooden slatted sides surrounding its bed sat in front of the house.

She looked to Tate. "If you have bought me a big, ugly truck for my wedding present after I bought you those gorgeous alligator-skin boots you are in *such* trouble."

He chuckled and pulled her to the back of the truck. "It's not about the truck. It's about what's in it." He pulled the tail gait open.

A sea of red met her gaze.

"Roses." The word was a bare whisper as tears sprang to her eyes. "Red roses."

There must have been fifty rose plants in the back of the truck. All in full bloom.

"And pansies. Don't forget the pansies." Tate pointed below the roses.

Trays and trays of purple and yellow pansies, their bright, cheery faces pointed toward the sky, sat beneath the canvas of red. Tears poured down her cheeks. She looked to Tate, her tall, dark, sweet, sweet cowboy. "How did you find blooming pansies in the fall?"

"I contacted the nursery as soon as we got back from the Bahamas. They grew them for you."

Tate had had them grown for her. He'd remembered the talk they'd had one quiet night and had them grown for her. So she could have the dream. She threw her arms around him and hugged him tight. "They're perfect. Thank you."

He hugged her back, then pulled back just far enough to see her face. "Your dad has left his mark all over this place. I thought it was time you and your mother did the same." He wiped the tears gently from her cheeks. "Where do you want them planted?"

"How 'bout behind the house? There's shade there."

He looked toward his house, their house, his brows

pulling together. "I thought we'd put the swing set out there."

She stilled. "The swing set?"

"Yeah. The swing set." Excitement sparkled in his eyes. "The kids have to have something to play on. They can't ride horses all day."

She couldn't believe her ears. "Kids?"

He gave her a beaming smile. "Oh, yeah, I want at least six of them. Didn't I mention that?"

Wonder flowed through her. She thought she'd pulled a miracle off when she'd convinced Tate to let her into his life. She hadn't dared to even think about children for fear she'd send him running. But he wasn't running now. He was grasping hold of their future and hanging on tight.

More tears flooded her eyes. She swiped them away. "A family. I like that idea. I like it a lot."

He kissed her, slow and tender. "It's going to be good, Crissy."

She touched her lips to his. "Yes, it is. It's going to be very, very good."

Good.

And wonderful.

And so, so bright.

* * * * *

Look for the next Alpine Angel story in 2005.

Coming in October 2004 from

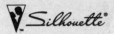

SPECIAL EDITION™

and author
Christine Rimmer

Marrying Molly

(Silhouette Special Edition #1639)

Salon owner Molly O'Dare vowed to never be
single and pregnant. That is, until a passionate
love affair landed her in both of these
categories. The child's father—wealthy and
dashingly handsome Tate Bravo—insisted on
marrying Molly. But she was determined to
resist until he could offer exactly what
she wanted: true love.

Stronger than ever...

Available at your favorite retail outlet.

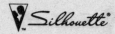

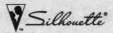

SPECIAL EDITION™

presents
a heartwarming NEW series!

THE HATHAWAYS
OF MORGAN CREEK:
A DYNASTY
IN THE BAKING...

NANNY IN HIDING

(SSE #1642, available October 2004)

by

Patricia Kay

On the run from her evil ex-husband, Amy Jordan
accepted blue-eyed Bryce Hathaway's offer to be his
children's nanny. This wealthy single dad was
immediately intrigued by the beautiful runaway, but if
he discovered that this caring, gentle woman was
actually a nanny *in hiding*, would he
help her out—or turn her in?

Available at your favorite retail outlet.

Receive a FREE hardcover book from

H A R L E Q U I N   R O M A N C E®

in September!

Harlequin Romance celebrates the launch of the line's new cover design by offering you this exclusive offer valid only in September, only in Harlequin Romance.

To receive your FREE HARDCOVER BOOK written by bestselling author Emilie Richards, send us four proofs of purchase from any September 2004 Harlequin Romance books. Further details and proofs of purchase can be found in all September 2004 Harlequin Romance books.

Must be postmarked no later than October 31.

Don't forget to be one of the first to pick up a copy of the new-look Harlequin Romance novels in September!

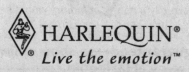

Visit us at www.eHarlequin.com

HRPOP0904

eHARLEQUIN.com

The Ultimate Destination for Women's Fiction

Visit eHarlequin.com's Bookstore today
for today's most popular books at great prices.

- An extensive selection of romance books by top authors!

- Choose our convenient "bill me" option. No credit card required.

- New releases, Themed Collections and hard-to-find backlist.

- A sneak peek at upcoming books.

- Check out book excerpts, book summaries and Reader Recommendations from other members and post your own too.

- Find out what everybody's reading in Bestsellers.

- Save BIG with everyday discounts and exclusive online offers!

- Our Category Legend will help you select reading that's exactly right for you!

- Visit our Bargain Outlet often for huge savings and special offers!

- Sweepstakes offers. Enter for your chance to win special prizes, autographed books and more.

Your purchases are 100% guaranteed—so shop online at www.eHarlequin.com today!

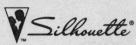

SPECIAL EDITION

#1639 MARRYING MOLLY—Christine Rimmer
Bravo Family Ties
Salon owner Molly O'Dare vowed to never be single *and* pregnant.
That is, until a passionate love affair landed her in both of these
categories. The child's father—wealthy and dashingly handsome
Tate Bravo—insisted on marrying Molly. But she was determined to
resist until he could offer exactly what she wanted: true love.

#1640 THE PRINCE'S BRIDE—Lois Faye Dyer
The Parks Empire
Wedding planner Emily Parks had long since given up her dream
of starting a family and decided to focus on her career. She never
imagined that the dashing Prince Lazhar Eban would ever want
her to be his bride, but little did she know that what began as a
business proposition would turn into the marriage proposal she'd
always dreamed of!

#1641 THE DEVIL YOU KNOW—Laurie Paige
Seven Devils
When Roni Dalton literally fell onto FBI agent Adam Smith's table
at a restaurant, she set off a chain of mutual passion that neither
could resist. Adam claimed that he was too busy to get involved, but
when he suddenly succumbed to their mutual attraction, Roni was
determined to change this self-proclaimed singleton into a
marriage-minded man.

#1642 NANNY IN HIDING—Patricia Kay
The Hathaways of Morgan Creek
On the run from her evil ex-husband, Amy Jordan accepted blue-
eyed Bryce Hathaway's offer to be his children's nanny. This
wealthy single dad was immediately intrigued by the beautiful
runaway, but if he discovered that this caring, gentle woman was
actually a nanny *in hiding,* would be help her out—or turn her in?

#1643 WRONG TWIN, RIGHT MAN—Laurie Campbell
Beth Montoya and her husband, Rafael, were on the verge of
divorce when Beth barely survived a brutal train accident. When she
was struck with amnesia and mistakenly identified as her
twin sister, Anne, Rafael offered to take care of "Anne" while she
recovered. Suddenly lost passion flared between them…but then her
true identity started to surface….

#1644 MAKING BABIES—Wendy Warren
Recently divorced Elaine Lowry yearned for a baby of her own.
Enter Mitch Ryder—sinfully handsome and looking for an heir to
carry on his family name. He insisted that their marriage be strictly
business, but what would happen if she couldn't hold up her end of
the deal?